AF487102

He burst out laughing, taking her hand in his before lifting it face up. Leaning down, he pressed his lips to the centre of her palm, saying, "You are not just beautiful, but damn sexy too. Will you dance with me?"

Her eyelashes fluttered rapidly as Shreya felt an emotion she had never, ever felt before in her life when a wave of shyness enveloped her. Lifting her heavy eyelids halfway to meet his dark gaze, she gave him a small nod, responding to him in a breathless voice, "Yes."

Chirag swept her into his arms to circle around the peripheral of the dance floor, his eyes holding hers firmly, not letting her look away from him. The Sagittarius man was hooked—at least for the moment—and he wanted to make sure this woman focused on him and no one else.

The Aquarius woman was impressed by the man's self-confidence, the way he held her close, but not too close; the way he teased, but not hurtfully; the way he drew her into a casual conversation, gleaning a lot of information about her.

ABOUT THE AUTHOR

Sundari Venkatraman is an Indie Author who has 72 books to her credit. These books have consistently featured in the Top 100 Bestseller Lists on Amazon Kindle, in both romance as well as Asian Drama categories. Her latest hot romances have all been on #1 Bestseller slot in Amazon India for over a month.

AQUARIUS REBEL is a hot romance novel and the sixth and final book in the Written in the Stars series. It can also be read as a standalone novel. This kindle book remained in the #1 Bestseller position on Amazon India for three months after its release.

Even as a child, Sundari absolutely loved the 'lived happily ever after' syndrome and she grew up on a steady diet of fairy tales, Phantom comics, and Mandrake comics. It was always about good triumphing over evil and a happy ending after the protagonists surmounted all unexpected obstacles.

Once she entered her teens, Sundari switched her loyalties from fairy tales to Mills & Boon. While she loved reading both, she kept visualising what would have happened if there were similar situations happening in India; to local heroes and heroines. And of course, the joy of vanquishing the ubiquitous evil villains! Her imagination soared and she happily ensconced herself in a rosy romantic cocoon for many years.

Then came the writing—a true bolt from the blue! And Sundari Venkatraman has never looked back.

Book list By Sundari Venkatraman

Standalone novels
The Malhotra Bride
Meghna
The Madras Affair
An Autograph for Anjali
Twin Torment
Finding Anya
Mr. Perfect
Man Friday
Her Prince Charming
Love in Agartha
Arjun's Penance
The Floundering Author
Ryan Finds a Bride
Tinder Loving Care
Shaan Gets Hitched
For Better or For Worse
Love… No Conditions Asked
Is This Love?
Press Restart

Collection of shorts
Matches Made in Heaven
Tales of Sunshine

Marriages Made in India Series
#1 The Runaway Bridegroom
#2 Her Smitten Husband
#3 His Drunken Wife
#4 Her Secret Husband
#5 The Casanova's Wife
#6 Her Bohemian Husband

The Bansal Legacy Trilogy
#1 Simha International
#2 Rose Garden International
#3 Maharaja International

The Thakore Royals Trilogy
#1 The Marriage Predicament
#2 Tied in Knots
#3 The Wooing of the Shrew

The Groom Series Trilogy
#1 Groomnapped
#2 Gobsmacked
#3 Grounded

Written in the Stars Series
#1 Scorpio Superstar
#2 Leo's Desire
#3 Taurus Temptation
#4 Virgo's Krush
#5 Libra's Flame
#6 Aquarius Rebel

Arora Iyers Trilogy
#1 Once Bitten Twice Lucky
#2 Heartthrob
#3 Call of the Heart

Dashavatar (Indian Mythology)
MATSYA: The First Avatar
KURMA: The Second Avatar
VARAHA: The Third Avatar
NARASIMHA: The Fourth Avatar
VAMANA: The Fifth Avatar
PARASHURAMA: The Sixth Avatar

**The Princess Series
(Historical Romance)**
#1 The Passionate Princess
#2 The Rebel Princess

**The Prince Series
(Historical Romance)**
#1 The Banished Prince

The Writer's Toolkit (Non-fiction)
Publishing Your Book on Amazon KDP

Bollywood Bros Trilogy
#1 Sing For Me
#2 Dance With Me
#3 Lights, Camera, Action!

Romantic Shorts
#1 *Chahti Hoon Tumhe*
#2 Beauty is but Skin Deep
#3 Madeinheaven.com
#4 An Arranged Match
#5 The Reluctant Bride
#6 *Shweta ka Swayamvar*
#7 Papa's Girl
#8 Red Rose Dating Agency
#9 Rahat Mili
#10 Reema's Matchmakers
#11 The Matchmaker's Dream

AQUARIUS
REBEL

WRITTEN IN THE STARS
BOOK 6

A Contemporary Romance Novel

SUNDARI VENKATRAMAN

FLAMING SUN

Notion Press Media Pvt Ltd
No. 50, Chettiyar Agaram Main Road,
Vanagaram, Chennai, Tamil Nadu – 600 095

First Published by Flaming Sun 2020
Printed & Distributed by Notion Press
Copyright © Sundari Venkatraman 2022 & 2025
All Rights Reserved.

ISBN 979-8-89777-105-9

Edited by: The Book Club Editorial Panel
Beta read by: Lakshmi Ranganathan
Cover Design by: Vivek Chandanshiv

Of the Aquarius-Sagittarius match...

If an astrologer could sum up planetary wisdom in one brief phrase, for counselling Sagittarius and Aquarius concerning the achievement of a smooth association together, it would be to advise both of them to make one powerful effort to remain calm, cool and collected, under any and all circumstances. Such a few words. But so vitally important to these two Earthlings. Sagittarius is a Fire Sign, therefore extremely volatile. When the Water Bearer (Aquarius is an Air Sign, remember) becomes a little windy and fans the Archer's fiery nature into flames – the resultant conflagration will whip the Aquarius Air into a regular tornado of fury.

– LINDA GOODMAN

Ambika and Sunil Udhas have great pleasure in inviting you to the wedding of their daughter SHREYA, with…

"Noooooo!"

His face draining of colour, Chirag Bhatia shouted the word as he forcefully threw his cell phone on the sofa in one corner of his office, not far from where he was standing at the window. His heart thumped heavily, sweat forming on his forehead and upper lip as he fumed. He had just got to know that Shreya, his girlfriend of four years, his fuck buddy, the woman he was having a long-distance affair with, was getting married. The invitation was a forward from her younger sister, Aadhira.

But why? How?

And no, Chirag didn't want to know the date, or the name of the man who was the bridegroom. That wasn't the reason for him to lose his cool.

Chirag had been sure that Shreya wasn't keen on marriage, same as himself. And she had all this long been thwarting all her mother's efforts to push her into wedded bliss.

While he lived in Delhi, India, she was based in Durban, South Africa. But the distance hadn't mattered during the four years they had known each other.

In the beginning, all Chirag had been interested in, was a brief fling. Shreya was not only beautiful with a gorgeous figure, but she was also extremely intelligent and Chirag had been totally drawn to her right from the start. He had been confident that their affair would run its course. But it hadn't, not even after four years.

Then why the hell had she agreed to marry some other man? Chirag was all set to blow his top. Agreed, he hadn't shown interest in tying the knot with her. But neither had she. If she had… Chirag paused for a few moments. *What would I have done if she had told me she was interested in getting married?*

He shook his head to himself, not very sure. Would he have offered to marry her? Was he ready for marriage? From the day Shreya entered his life, Chirag had not glanced at another woman, at least not in a flirtatious light. In fact, he had not even felt an urge to check out other women, young or old; beautiful or ugly; not after meeting Shreya.

Did that mean he was in love with her? Chirag did not know.

One thing he was clear about though—the roiling jealousy he felt at the pit of his abdomen, for the man who was planning to marry Shreya.

NO!!!

"Hey, is something wrong?" Nishaan Ahuja, Chirag's bestie from childhood, walked into the office cabin, startled to see the way Chirag punched his fist into a wall.

"Yes, damn it! My world has fallen apart," shouted Chirag, turning to glare at Nishaan as if it was all his fault.

"Eh? How come?"

"Shreya is getting married," said Chirag, his tone suggesting that the world was coming to an end indeed.

"So?" Managing to curb a smile, Nishaan gave his best friend a curious glance. He could read all the symptoms of a man in love in Chirag. Only, he had been denying it for all of four years. It looked like the time had come for Chirag to face the truth.

Chirag was all set to jump down Nishaan's throat. "What the hell do you mean by that? Didn't you hear what I said?"

Nishaan shrugged. "Of course, I did. You said that Shreya was getting married. But so what?"

Chirag reached across to catch Nishaan's jacket collar in both his hands, shaking him, not very successfully. "My Shreya is getting married," he shouted, his black eyes thunderous as he glared at the other man.

Nishaan clamped his hands around Chirag's forearms to pull his hands off his collar. "Is she? *Your* Shreya, I mean?"

"If you weren't my best friend, you'd be sporting a black eye by now," growled Chirag, stepping away from Nishaan, just so that he wasn't tempted to punch him. Such was the heat of his temper! Couldn't Nishaan see how terribly hurt he felt by what he saw as Shreya's duplicity? How could she go behind Chirag's back and get married? It was only six weeks ago when they had spent four blissful days roaming the streets of Paris, and spending each night making torrid love in their hotel room. She had not breathed a word to him of her plans even at that time. What kind of a woman did that make her? This was betrayal at its height!

He began pacing the length of the office, his face grim as he wondered about how to deal with the situation. That he still wanted Shreya was obvious. Their love affair was over by no means. And she couldn't simply walk out on him like this.

Nishaan plonked himself down on one of the visitors' chairs in front of Chirag's desk and called the office kitchen for some coffee and sandwiches. "I'm famished," he declared in the way of explanation when Chirag turned to glare at him with a raised eyebrow.

"Feel free," said Chirag, highly sarcastic. Not that it mattered. Nishaan was always welcome in his office and did not have to ask Chirag's permission for anything. But right now, Chirag needed a punching bag and Nishaan was available.

Nishaan didn't bother to respond to Chirag's sarcasm as he watched his friend pace the office angrily, a serene expression on his own face.

Chirag came over to sit in his swivel chair when the office boy brought a tray with coffee, along with cheese and chicken sandwiches. "Why are you so quiet?" he asked Nishaan.

Nishaan shrugged. "Don't want to disturb you as you seem deep in thought."

"Deep in thought, my ass," growled Chirag, keeping his coffee mug down violently, uncaring when some of the beverage sloshed over into the tray. "I'm going to kill Shreya with my bare hands," he snarled some more.

"To what purpose?" asked Nishaan calmly, an eyebrow rising in query as he glanced at his best friend's enraged face.

"Huh?" Chirag frowned at Nishaan, trying to wrap his head around the latter's words. Finally comprehending, he snapped, "Just for the pleasure of it."

"I thought humping Shreya gave you pleasure enough. What has changed?" asked Nishaan, biting into a sandwich with relish.

Chirag, who had picked up his coffee mug once again, paused in the middle of carrying it to his lips, to glower at Nishaan. "Do you think it's funny?" he bit out.

Nishaan shook his head. "Of course not. I'm only trying to understand the situation here. You never wanted to marry Shreya, did you?" he asked gently.

Chirag swallowed the coffee with difficulty as he felt something clog his throat, unfamiliar with the emotion driving him. Realising that he might gag if he had more of the beverage, he returned the mug once again to the tray and stared at Nishaan unseeingly. Suddenly recalling that the other man was expecting an answer from him, he said, "I don't know, *yaar*. I really don't know."

Chirag had never associated Shreya and marriage in his life. But then, he had been having so much fun with her that he had not given marriage a thought. Luckily, his parents hadn't either. It was a good thing he was the youngest of three children, and a male at that. His parents had been busy getting their daughters married off; and later, helping them with the birth of their children. Chirag had three nephews and one niece from his two sisters.

Nishaan glanced at the pathetic expression on Chirag's face, feeling rather sorry for him. He could make out that his friend was on the verge of discovering that he had fallen in love with the woman he had been having an affair with. That the relationship had lasted for more than four years must have told Chirag something before now. But it was obvious that Chirag had chosen not to give the prolonged time frame too much thought. And despite being Chirag's closest friend, Nishaan didn't think it was his place to point things out to the other man. Nishaan was sure he didn't want his head bitten off for his efforts. The funny part was that Chirag was the one with the sunny nature. But he appeared driven just now, all set to explode in frustration.

"Want to go for a drink?" asked Nishaan.

Chirag stared at Nishaan, a faraway expression in his eyes. Right now, he wanted to be alone as he tackled his abject misery at what he considered to be Shreya's treachery. Forgetting all about Nishaan, he went to get his phone from where it was lying on the corner sofa to check the date of her wedding. A deep sigh shuddered through his lean frame when he saw it was to be held after three months, and in Durban. He scrolled up the invite to see if there was any information about the bridegroom. He clenched his jaw hard when he noticed that it was someone called Reyansh Bhargav based in Durban itself. Grr!

"Chirag?" Nishaan tried to garner his friend's attention.

Chirag looked up from his phone blankly, as if wondering what Nishaan was doing in his office. Suddenly recalling that the latter wanted to go out for a drink, he said, "You go on, *yaar*. I'm not in the mood," his mouth drooping at the corners.

Nishaan was torn, wondering if he should leave Chirag alone in this melancholic mood. But then, he respected that the other man wanted to be by himself. The reason why Nishaan had gone over to Chirag's office was to share some news from his side; that he and his long-time girlfriend Chaahat Wadhwa, had finally set a date for their wedding. But Nishaan realised that the present time was not the right one to share his good news with his best friend. It will wait, as the date was set for two months from now.

"If you're sure," said Nishaan, getting up. He walked across to Chirag and patted his shoulder. "I'm sure things will work out for the best."

"From when did you become a philosopher?" asked Chirag, glowering at the other man.

Nishaan gave him a grin. "From the day I met my match." And he left.

Chirag jumped to his feet, his mind working in a frenzied fashion. His friend Nishaan Ahuja had been a gay bachelor; actually, he still was. Only, these days he had a steady girlfriend in Chaahat. In fact, Nishaan and Chaahat had been together for five years, all because the two of them were in love. They were even planning to tie the knot soon.

He paced back and forth, a deep frown on his forehead. "I don't want to be disturbed," he snarled when someone knocked on his door before opening it. Seeing his second-in-command, the vice president of his company, he barked, "Go home, Vikrant. I want to think." He didn't bother to find out if Vikrant followed his order as he continued to wear down the carpet with his furious pacing.

"Are you sure, boss?" asked Vikrant, stepping inside to stand next to the door, his legs at ease, and his massive arms crossed over his equally massive chest. While his eyes smiled, he kept his expression stern as he looked at Chirag. The two men went a long way, and had become friends over the years.

Chirag stopped pacing to glare at Vikrant. "About what?" he snarled.

"You're being rude."

Chirag sighed, extra loudly. "What do you want?"

It was nothing very important, and Vikrant didn't want to bother his boss about it, not when it was obvious that Chirag was upset about something. "Forget it. I think there's trouble in paradise?" asked Vikrant, lifting a thick eyebrow in query.

"Do you think it's any of your business?" asked Chirag, going to stand in front of the younger man. They both were equally tall and big built as they stood toe to toe.

"The last time that happened, it was my business," said Vikrant, giving Chirag a cheeky smile.

"Just go, Vik." Chirag quietened down to speak softly.

"Want some advice?" asked Vikrant.

"Will it be of any use if I tell you that I don't?" Right now, Chirag wouldn't mind the other man's advice—after all, Vikrant Bakshi was extremely adept at trouble shooting.

Vikrant laughed softly. "Why don't you put yourself out of misery and make Shreya Udhas your wife?" His words were gentle, but spoken in a firm voice.

The colour disappeared from Chirag's face, leaving it pale and haggard. "You seriously think so?" he asked, a stunned expression in his eyes.

"Of course, yes, Chirag. Why will I tell you so if I didn't believe it's the solution for your unhappiness?"

"Why did you never tell me before, you bastard?" asked Chirag, a pathetic expression on his face. The few times the thought had arisen in him—that maybe he wanted a more permanent relationship with Shreya—he had squashed it mercilessly, every time.

"Why? Because I would like my head to continue to remain attached to my neck; and I would like to keep my job too; in that order. I'll see you, boss." Vikrant took an about turn and would have left the cabin, only to stop when he heard Chirag's anxiously whispered words.

"But it looks like it's too late."

"What? Why?" Vikrant turned right back to face Chirag.

"Her marriage is already fixed with someone else," said Chirag, his voice bitter as he stared unseeingly at the wall.

"Oh!" Vikrant's eyes went wide in shock. Thinking on his feet, he said, "When is the wedding?"

"In three months."

"There's still time then." There was utter relief on Vikrant's face as he looked eagerly at his CEO.

"For what?" Chirag looked at the other man with dull eyes.

"To stop that wedding and marry her yourself." Vikrant spoke in an enthusiastic voice. "All the best, boss," he said, before leaving the cabin.

Chirag plonked down on the visitors' chair which was closest to him, burying his face in his hands. Is that what he wanted to do? To make Shreya his wife? He thought of his best friend Nishaan Ahuja. Nishaan was in a happy space—had been from the time he met Chaahat.

Chirag lifted his face suddenly to stare at the door. He had met Shreya four years ago, and had not looked at another woman after that. Chirag, the man who used to flirt with women of all ages, one who had always had only brief love affairs, had stopped giving other women a second glance. All because Shreya had become the centre of his existence.

And today, receiving the news of her forthcoming marriage, had shaken Chirag to the core of his being. How much ever he wanted to blame Shreya, he didn't really have the right, did he? He had made no promises to her. Nor had she made any to him. There was no commitment between the two of them, as they met whenever they could and had fun, both in and out of bed.

But that still didn't stop him from feeling as if she had made a fool of him. Worse than that, he felt such a deep and unfamiliar anguish in the region of his chest, as if his heart was being squeezed, hard.

Chirag gasped loudly, when his mind threw up the most bizarre possibility. No, he wouldn't admit even to himself that this was not the first time he had thought about this being the case.

Have I fallen in love?

F*our years ago…*

"Shreya, how can you?" Ambika Udhas smote her forehead as she glared at her eldest child who was all of twenty-two. The girl had no sense it seemed.

"How can I what?" asked Shreya as a small scowl brought her shapely eyebrows together, not taking her eyes off her phone where she was chatting furiously with a friend on WhatsApp.

"*Arre*, look at yourself!" Ambika pressed her fists against her generous hips, continuing to frown at Shreya. "What will people think?"

"Who are these people? Tell them not to think, Mom!" Finally lifting her big brown eyes up to look at her mother, Shreya asked, "Do you think I really give a rat's ass for people's opinions?" A mischievous smile lit up the younger woman's face, for the Aquarius kowtowed to no one. Clad in the briefest of denim shorts which displayed her slim and long legs, paired with a bubble-gum pink sleeveless vest, she knew what her mother was upset about—her brief attire.

Ambika had become a different person altogether from the time they arrived in Delhi. What had been perfectly fine back home in Durban, was all wrong in

Delhi it seemed. It was always about what the neighbours will think. As for the relatives, her mother was sure that they would be flabbergasted by her children's clothes and behaviour which were too frivolous for Delhi society.

Duh!

"Shreya!" Ambika shouted her daughter's name. "Are you mad? How can you talk like that? Your Dad and I are working so hard to find you a nice bridegroom. The least you can do is dress decently. Don't you have any *salwar kameez* to wear?" The question was redundant as Ambika had made sure her daughter's wardrobe consisted of enough Indian formal wear. After all, how could she let the families of prospective bridegrooms see Shreya in shorts and vest?

"Don't be ridiculous, Mom. There's no one visiting us now. So, what's your problem? Can't I chill in my own home?" Shreya sat up straight before crossing her legs as she spoke to her mother. At five feet, five inches, she was completely fit. And how would she not be, as she taught yoga at a studio in Durban? She actively did yoga for at least three of the six hours she played instructor; the rest of the time was spent in ensuring that her students followed her steps correctly. Having been conscious of her figure right from when she was a plump teenager, Shreya had worked really hard to gain her presently slender form. At fourteen, it had not been too difficult to lose weight and inches with a strict diet and exercise. The challenge had been in maintaining her figure and keeping her weight in control. After trying out many methods, she had finally zeroed in on yoga which kept her not only fit and slim, but healthy too. Having trained for two years under a British couple living in Durban, she had joined a studio as an instructor. Her dream was to set up her own yoga centre, and she was saving money for the same.

"I suppose." Finally conceding to Shreya's stronger will, Ambika looked at her beautiful child, feeling a rush of pride when she took in her thick, dark, and luxurious hair with gold highlights, the smooth oval of her face with the biggest possible brown eyes which reminded one of fresh honey. Her nose was slim and sharp, exactly centred between her soft cheeks, her lips a rosy pink. The mother's temper rose again when her gaze landed on Shreya's cleavage. "Can't you wear something decent?"

Shreya, who had returned her attention to her phone, continued to type with both her thumbs as she responded in a bored voice. "I just thought we finished with that conversation." Lifting her gaze back to her mother, she scoffed, "Don't you have anything to do, Mom? I think you're bored."

Ambika took an about turn and walked into the kitchen to harass the cook. The middle-aged Tina had travelled to Durban along with Ambika twenty-eight years ago when the latter had moved to her husband's home soon after her marriage. When Ambika tasted all the dishes prepared for lunch and found something wanting in every one of them, Tina threw down the ladle and turned to her mistress, her temper flaring. "*Madamji, kuch takleef hai aapko?* Do you want me to quit this job?" she asked, fixing her accusing gaze on her mistress. This wouldn't be the first time they were arguing in the last three decades they had known each other.

"*Arre, itna badakti kyun ho?* What did I tell you? Only to make sure everything tastes perfect. Why should you leave your job for that?"

Tina noticed the niggling worry in her employer's eyes and calmed down immediately. "Let me make some tea, okay? We both can drink it together," Tina offered, as if she was bestowing an honour on Ambika.

"Is there anything to munch with it?" After all, there were two hours to go before lunch.

"I baked some almond cookies last night. And also made some spicy *shankarpali*, just the way you like it." Tina gave the other woman a dazzling smile as she made the tempting offer.

Ambika gave a long and loud sigh as she patted Tina's shoulder. "Bring them all to the living room. I'll wait for you there."

"*Ji Madamji.*"

"Will you join us for tea?" Ambika called out to Shreya who was sitting at the far end of the hall, still on her phone.

Tina placed the heavy tray on the centre table, before plopping herself into a straight-backed chair right next to Ambika where the latter languished on a sofa.

"Sure." Shreya got up to join the two older women, eyeing the tea tray. "Is there coffee?" she asked, preferring it to tea. "What else have you made, Tina *di*?" she asked, her eyes going wide as she looked at the snacks.

Tina gave Shreya a wide smile. "Of course there is coffee," she said, pouring it from a flask and handing the mug to Shreya. "And go on, try the snacks. I promise you that you'll love them."

"Are you trying to make me put on weight?" That didn't exactly stop Shreya from helping herself from the plate of almond cookies. "This is so damn yummy. You made?" she asked Tina, biting into a cookie with relish.

Ambika answered for Tina. "Of course it was Tina who baked the biscuits. That too, only last night. As for you putting on weight, I'm sure you can afford to add a few kilos, *beta*. You are so slim."

Shreya shuddered. "No way, Mom. You know how difficult it was to lose all my excess fat. Now that I'm at my optimum weight, I don't plan to gain even a hundred grams. But that doesn't mean I won't relish Tina *di's* cooking." Giving the cook a broad wink, she grabbed some *shankarpali* and munched on them. "Mmm… these are even better."

Tina gave Shreya a wide smile as she herself drank tea, not bothering to eat any snack. The cook didn't want to stuff herself, not before lunch.

Shreya glared at her image in the mirror, hating the *salwar kameez* from the bottom of her heart. It was not only a torrid rani pink, but also heavily embroidered with gold sequins, of all things. Where the hell had her mother found this costume? If Ambika had taken Shreya shopping, she would never have wasted money on this ugly set of clothes. Ugh!

But then, Ambika knew her daughter only too well, and had gone with a couple of her relatives to Chandni Chowk to purchase the outfit, confident that the colour would suit Shreya's fair complexion. She was not exactly wrong in thinking that. But it was made of some synthetic fabric and so heavily embroidered that Shreya cringed. While she argued with her mother *ad nauseum*, she didn't want to hurt her. And frankly, she didn't really care that she was wearing the outfit as they were going to a party full of strangers.

Her mother's attempt at finding her eldest born a groom was to inform everyone she met in Delhi that she was doing exactly that—searching for a suitable bridegroom. One of her friends, Rekha—working hard to establish herself as a marriage facilitator—had suggested that Nishaan Ahuja would make Shreya a perfect match. Today, Nishaan's parents—Aadharsh and Nalini Ahuja—were throwing a house party. Rekha had managed to wangle an invitation for Shreya and her parents—an informal way to meet a prospective bridegroom.

Eow!

While Shreya generally fell in with her mother's plans, she had absolutely no intention of getting married, not in the foreseeable future; and especially not if it was going to be arranged for her by others. While she had tried her best to dissuade her mother from making this trip to India for the purpose of finding Shreya a suitable bridegroom, Ambika had been insistent. Ambika had grabbed the opportunity to spend time in India with the family as her husband Sunil Udhas had an official project which made it necessary for him to be in Delhi for at least two months.

And here they were, the whole family—Sunil, Ambika, Shreya and her three younger siblings, Aadhira, Aryan, and Sumit—ensconced in a service apartment in Delhi, along with Tina.

Shreya opened the jewellery box on her dressing table, her eyes going wide in shock as she examined the contents. Was her mother serious about wanting her to wear all these ugly necklaces and heavy *jhumkas*? Like really! She shuddered when she removed a thick necklace in a paisley pattern studded with diamonds.

Yuck! She looked into the mirror when she noticed three faces peeping into the room.

"Come on in," she invited her siblings.

Sumit, all of thirteen years, and the youngest of the lot, stared at his older sister. "What is it that you are wearing?" he asked, lifting his horrified gaze to Shreya. "It looks ugly."

Seventeen-year-old Aryan nodded his curly head vigorously. "I agree with Sumit. Why the hell are you wearing something so… so gross?" he asked, wrinkling his nose. "Hey, are you going to wear these too?" he asked, picking up a gold and diamond *jhumka*.

Aadhira stepped behind the two to look at her older sister. "I think Shreya has a plan here," she said. Three years younger to Shreya, she was all admiration for her older sister's intelligence. "This is one surefire way to get the guy to run in the opposite direction. Is that what you are trying to achieve?"

"You think so?" Shreya responded to Aadhira first, turning to her eagerly.

"I think what? That the prospective groom will run away in the opposite direction? Most definitely, yes. But I don't know if that's what you are trying to achieve," Aadhira told her, her eyes dancing mischievously.

Shreya grinned. "Okay, you've convinced me." Turning to Aryan and Sumit, she said, "I'm wearing a *salwar kameez*, which is considered traditional here. And…"

"But still, Shrey, need it be so hideous?" Aryan shouted in protest, rolling his eyes.

"Mom seems to think it is *the* outfit to wear to this party. And yes, Aryan, I'm wearing those *jhumkas*."

"I hope the guy doesn't keel over in shock," grimaced Aryan, before giving Shreya a grin.

She slapped his arm, laughing. "Okay, I think this is it. I'll go to the party as if I'm a jewellery tree. Yuck!" She quickly wore the long chain around her neck before fitting the heavy earrings to her lobes. "Some heavy make-up?" she asked her siblings.

"Go for it," they choroused, watching her avidly as she applied a thick coating of foundation before a couple of layers of powder from her compact. She finished off with shocking pink eye shadow and a deeper shade of the same colour on her lips. Turning around, she lifted an eyebrow at her audience of three. "Will I do?"

Aryan lifted one shoulder in a half shrug. "What a waste of time and effort!"

Aadhira gave a suggestion. "I hope you're planning to carry a change of outfit."

"You think?" asked Shreya, her eyes slowly lighting up.

"Of course. It's a party, after all. There must be a lot of young people there. Don't you want to have at least a bit of fun?"

"You are bright, Aadhi, you are. I think I'll do just that."

"Promise me you won't get arrested," said Sumit.

"Eh? I don't get you."

"What if the guy dies of shock?" her youngest sibling asked, giving her a solemn wink.

"If that happens, I'm going to need the spare set of clothes all the more. I can change quickly and run away from the scene. Even better that no one will recognise me." She grimaced as she quickly packed a tote bag, adding the empty jewellery box to it; and not forgetting to throw in a shoe box as well. "Time to go," she said, straightening her shoulders.

Her siblings waved her off with last-minute suggestions and teasing words before Shreya went to meet her parents who were waiting for her in the hall.

"You look so beautiful, my child," said Ambika, her eyes shining with unshed tears.

Sunil stared at his daughter; not sure if he liked the way Shreya appeared. But he didn't dare utter a word as he wasn't keen to set his wife off, as Ambika had a tendency to rant.

"Let's go, then."

Shreya didn't lift her gaze to look at anyone, feeling truly ridiculous in her outfit. The only good thing was that there was not a single person at the Ahujas' home whom she had met before. She stood quietly next to her parents when Rekha, the common friend of both the Udhas and Ahuja families, made the introductions.

"You are so beautiful," said Nalini Ahuja, giving Shreya an adoring smile.

"Thank you, Aunty," said Shreya politely, continuing to look at her feet. They were going to have a *ghazal* programme in the lawn it seemed. She wanted to groan, feeling bored already.

"What would you like to have? Some wine? Or a cocktail?" Nishaan Ahuja, the prospective bridegroom she was here to meet, asked her.

"Do you have a *pina colada*?" asked Shreya, refusing to look at him.

"Of course." He was away for a few minutes before he came back to hand her the drink before saying, "Would you like to dance? We have a DJ playing at the back of the house."

She gave a nod before going along with him when he took her hand in his. She didn't miss the lack of chemistry and wasn't really surprised by that. She only hoped that Nishaan wasn't interested in her either.

As they walked into the living room of the bungalow, Nishaan asked, "Shreya, listen, do you know why you are here?"

She nodded, still refusing to look at him. She didn't want her mother being told that the man had refused her because of Shreya's rude behaviour. No, that wouldn't do at all. Ambika would never forgive her if such a thing happened.

"I'm not interested in the marriage. I love someone else…"

Shreya looked up at him, a stunned expression on her heavily painted face. Clutching his arm, she said, "Please tell me you mean it."

"What?" Nishaan appeared confused as he looked at Shreya's face for the first time. She appeared beautiful, despite her formal attire and heavy jewellery and heavier make-up. But she definitely was not for him.

"That you aren't interested in me and you love someone else." Shreya continued to hold his arm, pinning him with her brown gaze.

He laughed softly. "I mean it, of course. My girlfriend should be arriving soon."

Shreya gurgled with laughter, a tremendous feeling of relief overcoming her. "I can kiss you for that," she said, grinning at him, "in fact, I think I'll do exactly that." She took his face in her hands before going on the tips of her toes—he was so tall—and pressed her lips to his cheek. "You made my day. Where is the washroom?" she asked, determined to change into the party clothes she had carried along with her.

Nishaan pointed to the opposite corner. "Through there."

"Give me a few minutes and I would love to go partying after that." She went into the washroom and was glad to see that it was big and had a dry area. She quickly changed out of her *salwar kameez*; removing all the jewellery before packing them carefully in the box she had brought along. Changing into a short black dress which she felt so comfortable in, she quickly washed her face thoroughly before applying a coat of powder and nude gloss. Attaching a pair of silver hoops to her ears, she pulled her hair open from its plait and brushed it well before leaving it loose. Finally, she removed the *mojiris* from her feet before thrusting them into the black pumps she had brought along. There, she was ready! Pushing all her stuff into the tote bag, she walked out of the bathroom and on towards Nishaan, who was standing around chatting and laughing with another man.

"Hi again," she greeted Nishaan, realising that he didn't recognise her; grinning when his eyes went wide in surprise after a few moments.

"Hey, I almost didn't recognise you. You look so amazing. Not that you didn't before. But..."

The smile disappeared from Shreya's face, her gaze turning wary. "You haven't forgotten what you told me a few minutes ago, have you?"

Both the men laughed.

Shreya felt drawn to the handsome hunk standing next to Nishaan, wondering who he was. Part of the attraction was the fact that the man was not in her mother's radar as a suitable life partner for Shreya.

"Oh, by the way, this is my friend Chirag. And Chirag, this is Shreya." Nishaan performed the introductions, still grinning.

"Hey!" Chirag studied the woman in front of him, the rest of the world disappearing from around him as he had eyes only for her. "Where have you been hiding all my life?"

Shreya laughed flirtatiously. "In South Africa."

"Oh really! How interesting." Chirag took her elbow in his hand and guided her towards the other room, forgetting all about Nishaan. "Could I help you with that bag you're carrying? You can pick it up later."

"Oh, that would be perfect," she said, handing the tote to Chirag.

Chirag turned to Nishaan, handing the bag over to him.

Nishaan lifted an eyebrow, his eyes dancing with mischief.

"Please, *yaar*," mouthed Chirag.

Nishaan gave a nod before accepting the bag and leaving the couple alone.

Turning back to Shreya, Chirag invited, "Come along."

Shreya took the hand he proffered and went with him to the back of the house where people were dancing to a DJ. "This is so cool," she declared, having been under the impression that it was going to be a *ghazal* evening at the Ahujas' home. "Someone mentioned *ghazal*," she said, shuddering.

Chirag laughed, leaning down to speak close to her ear as the noise level was high. "I know, right? But it's a mixed crowd of youngsters and oldies."

She grimaced. "I see." She looked around, wondering if she could get something to drink. She felt parched, having left her *pina colada* somewhere along the way, after taking barely a sip from it.

"Do you want to have something to drink?" he asked, reading her expression correctly. By God! She was beautiful. Working all kinds of hours running his advertising agency, Chirag Bhatia had been too busy to find time for a girlfriend. Exactly the reason why Sukriti, his girlfriend of eight months, had dumped him some time last year.

"Yes, please. What I need is something long and cool!"

"Beer?" he offered with a lifted eyebrow.

"Perfect, thanks," she grinned.

Taking her hand in his, he pulled her to the other end of the room, determined not to lose her. Taller than many of the people standing at the bar, he lifted a hand to one of the barmen, and showed two fingers.

Reading his order correctly, the barman picked up two cans of beer from a crate of ice and handed them over to Chirag.

"Thanks, man." Chirag opened one can and handed it to Shreya who took a long swig from it before smacking her lips.

"This is good," she said, drinking some more.

"Another?" Chirag watched her in fascination. She was slugging beer like a pro.

"Yes, please."

He laughed, getting one more beer before taking her hand and walking to a far corner. He had a reason for it as he had noticed at least four other men eyeing Shreya avidly, and Chirag was in no mood to share her with anyone. At least, not until he got to know her. Far away from the speakers, they could at least hear one another without shouting.

"So, your parents are on the lookout for a groom for you?" Chirag worded it as a question even though he had it on Nishaan's authority that that was why they had come to this party—to find out the suitability of Nishaan as Shreya's groom.

"Tch! *Nasha uthar gaya!* Now you will have to get me more of this," grumbled Shreya, giving him a miffed glance.

"Eh? And why is that?" asked Chirag, not bothering to move from where he was standing, leaning against the wall.

"Why did you have to remind me of the reason my parents brought me here?" She gave him a mock glare before finishing her beer.

"Shouldn't I have?" he asked, his eyes crinkling at the corners as he smiled at her.

He was so damn handsome! With a lithe body too. The powder blue linen jacket was obviously not padded at his shoulders, hugging their width so lovingly too. His V-shaped body tapered down to a lean waist, and his muscular legs, encased in cream-coloured cotton pants, seemed to go on forever.

"Will I do?" asked Chirag, his smile growing wider. He liked the way she was studying him with her big brown eyes, so boldly too.

"Eh?" She lifted her gaze from his large feet encased in brown leather moccasins to meet his black-as-coal gaze. Light colour ran on her slim cheeks even as she gave him a smile. "Oh yes, you will."

"Hahahaha!" Chirag burst out laughing, liking her a lot by now. Bold and beautiful! His kind of woman. "You didn't answer my earlier question."

"Aren't you persistent?"

"I suppose I am."

"My parents—at least my mother, more than my father—are keen to get me married off," she grimaced.

"I suppose you aren't." It was a statement, not a question. Chirag thanked the waiter who had brought a couple of more beers for them.

"How did you manage that?" she asked, impressed and grateful for more beer.

"No big deal," he shrugged, waiting for her to answer.

With a dramatic sigh, she said, "Of course I am not. Who wants to get married so early in life?" She shuddered.

"You mean you are here under false pretences?" he asked, an expression of mock horror on his face, even as he wondered how old she was.

She pouted at him. "Very funny."

"Why not tell them you don't want to get married so soon?"

She rolled her eyes. "Seriously? What about your parents, Chirag? Don't they want to get you married off?"

He shrugged. "I don't know. We haven't really got around to discussing that."

"Aren't you lucky? How come?"

He laughed. "I have two sisters, older than me. My parents are still reeling from the effect of getting both of them married off." He crossed his fingers at his side as he uttered those words.

"I am the oldest sister in my family," she said, giving him an accusing stare as if it was all his fault.

He laughed some more. "How many siblings?"

"Two brothers and one sister."

"Are they back home in South Africa?"

"Nope. They are all right here in Delhi. Just in case I need to get married at short notice," she said, grimacing.

"Eh? You might have to do that?" His eyebrow lifted to touch the lock of thick hair which had fallen on his forehead.

She curled her hand into a fist when she felt a sudden urge to touch that lock of hair, just to know if it was really as silky as it appeared. Shrugging at his question, she said, "That's what my mother thinks."

He shook his head, deciding to change the subject as it was obvious that the talk of marriage irritated her. "So, what do you do, Shreya? Are you still studying?"

"Oh, that was years ago. These days, I am a yoga instructor in Durban."

"Which is where you live." He ran his eyes quickly down her lush figure before lifting it up, this time slowly as he took his time studying her perfectly curved, sexy body. The top of her head barely reached his shoulder despite the heels she wore. For such a slim woman, her breasts were lush—definitely a 34C. He finally lifted his gaze to meet her eyes which had darkened to a shade of molten honey and gave her a smile.

"Will I do?" she asked, her voice a tad breathless. She hadn't expected his gaze to make her grow so hot and bothered, which was a first. Shreya had had her share of boyfriends, strictly for dating. So far, she had not felt the urge to sleep with any of them. And this was the first time she felt her pulse rate go crazy at a man's gaze on her. She made a mental note to remain wary of Chirag.

He burst out laughing, taking her hand in his before lifting it face up. Leaning down, he pressed his lips to the centre of her palm, saying, "You are not just beautiful, but damn sexy too. Will you dance with me?"

Her eyelashes fluttered rapidly as Shreya felt an emotion she had never, ever felt before in her life when a wave of shyness enveloped her. Lifting her heavy eyelids halfway to meet his dark gaze, she gave him a small nod, responding to him in a breathless voice, "Yes."

Chirag swept her into his arms to circle around the peripheral of the dance floor, his eyes holding hers firmly, not letting her look away from him. The Sagittarius man was hooked—at least for the moment—and he wanted to make sure this woman focused on him and no one else.

The Aquarius woman was impressed by the man's self-confidence, the way he held her close, but not too close; the way he teased, but not hurtfully; the way he drew her into a casual conversation, gleaning a lot of information about her.

"And what do you do, Chirag?" she asked, never taking her gaze off his, for she needed to concentrate really hard to distract herself from the way her body clung to his, her right palm pressed to his left, their fingers firmly locked together.

"I run an advertising agency," he responded, his gaze moving down to her lips as she bit the luscious lower one with her small, white teeth, the gesture making him grow hard with longing.

"Your own? Wow!" She was impressed.

He shrugged, swinging her around the dance floor, glad of the slow music which made it possible for them to dance together as a couple. "Yep."

"You must have a lot of people working for you."

"Hmm… mmm."

"Don't you like to talk about your work?" she asked, scowling at his not very enthusiastic response.

"I don't want to bore you," he protested. "I would rather talk about you."

She laughed softly, shaking her head. "I don't get bored, ever. There! You know something more about me."

He threw back his head and laughed.

She stopped dancing as the music came to an end, and watched him in fascination. What would it be like to be kissed by this handsome dude? She couldn't wait to find out. But suddenly, out of the blue, her stomach growled loudly. At least, it sounded so loud to her.

"You're hungry. Come along, let's go find some food." Wrapping his arm around her slim waist, he turned her towards the doorway. "The buffet is out in the garden."

She grimaced, not at all keen to go where her parents must be. But well, it looked like she didn't have much of a choice.

Extremely observant, Chirag noticed the unhappy expression on her face. "I'm sure everyone must be at the *ghazal* programme. The buffet is at the other end."

She gave him a dazzling smile. "Lead the way."

And he did that, a broad grin on his handsome face.

Ambika had a lot to say to her daughter on their way home. "What's with this short dress?" she glared at her daughter, her temper coming to the fore when she noticed Shreya's changed clothing only after getting into the car.

Shreya, who had expected to be criticised, had got into the car before calling her father, telling him that she was ready to go home. "Why Mom? This is what people wear to parties, even here in Delhi."

Ambika couldn't really argue with that as she had noticed girls of Shreya's age wearing even briefer clothing. Grimacing, she asked, "Where did you disappear to? I hope you spent time with Nishaan."

Shreya gave an audible sigh. "Mom, Nishaan is not interested in me."

"How do you know?" Ambika was quick to argue. "His mother is searching for a suitable bride for him."

Shreya shrugged. "Maybe she is. But he is already in love with someone."

"Oh! So, that's how it is. I did wonder who that Chaahat was, the woman he was holding hands with." Turning to her husband who was sitting in the front, next to the driver, she said, "I have a good mind to pick a fight with Rekha. How can she do this to us? Make us meet the Ahujas when their son is already interested in some other girl? What a waste of time!"

Sunil shrugged. "Not exactly a waste of time, my dear. I got to make a lot of useful contacts. And maybe even some friends."

"Tch! It's always about your business," she grumbled.

"Why? Didn't you enjoy the *ghazal* programme?" he asked in a pacifying voice.

"It was nice, I suppose." Ambika's lips drooped unhappily. After all, the purpose of why they had gone there, was lost.

"And the food was excellent," continued Sunil enthusiastically. Turning to his daughter, he asked, "Did you have fun, *beta*?" He smiled when her eyes lit up brilliantly.

Shreya managed to shut her eyes before her mother could notice her excitement. She didn't want Ambika to chase her to get married to Chirag Bhatia now; as neither of them—Chirag nor Shreya—had any plans of getting married, either to each other or to someone else. "It wasn't bad, Dad. After I changed out of those ridiculous clothes and jewellery, of course."

"Humph!" Ambika had the last word.

3

"Hey, good time to talk?"

It was five in the evening when hearing it ping, Shreya opened her phone to read the WhatsApp message from Chirag, a smile spreading on her face. She called him immediately. "Hey."

"Hello! How have you been?"

"Not too bad. And you?"

"Alright, I suppose. Wanna meet for drinks and dinner?" He came directly to the point. It was two days after the party and Chirag found himself thinking of Shreya more often than not. It had been fun guzzling beers with her as they danced and chatted at Nishaan's home. And dinner with her had been pleasant, though they had had no privacy at all, not after leaving the dance floor and going to the garden. And now, he wanted to know her more.

"What time?" Wouldn't she love to meet Chirag! He was not just handsome, but such delightful company too.

"Shall I pick you up at seven?" he asked.

She scrunched up her nose, thinking quickly on her feet. "Can't I meet you somewhere?"

"Why?" he teased, a smile in his voice, "You don't want me to meet your family?" he asked.

"It's more like I don't want my mother to meet you. Unless you want her to truss you up and carry you over to take your *saat phere* along with me at the soonest." She gurgled with laughter as she visualised the scene.

"Ouch! I get what you mean. Let me see. What kind of food do you want to eat?"

"*Desi khana*, ideally something off the street. Do you mind?"

He was surprised at her choice, but kept that opinion to himself. "Are you ready to dare the crowds of Chandni Chowk?"

"How bad can it be?" she asked.

"Are you telling me you haven't been there?"

"Maybe more than a decade ago. But I can't remember."

"Okay, Chandini Chowk it is. You can have all kinds of street food there."

"Why don't you give me your address? I'll come over."

"What if my parents have something to say about that?" he teased, laughing.

"Are you serious?" She was frowning now. One set of parents was more than enough to deal with.

He guffawed. "Nope. Let me give you my office address. You get here around six. Works?"

"Perfect. I'll see you there."

Shreya was eager to see his place of work, mainly because it was his own set up. She wondered how big it was. Advertising, he had said. She opened her phone to see the message when it pinged, whistling when she noted the address Chirag had sent—World Trade Tower, New Barakhamba Road, Connaught Place. "Take the metro," he had mentioned, giving more directions. "Or you might get caught in traffic."

"See you soon," she responded with a smile on her face.

She quickly showered before donning a pair of ragged jeans which stopped two inches short of her ankle, admiring the holes over both her knees and a tear at the hem. Perfect! She paired it with a pastel yellow cotton top which was short, the hem barely touching the waist of her jeans. Brushing her hair thoroughly, she pulled it up into a high pony, applying a touch of eyeliner and lipstick. Clipping a pair of yellow plastic hoop earrings to her ears, Shreya added her cell phone, house keys, some tissues, her wallet, and a tube of lipstick to a denim sling bag before wearing it over her left shoulder and across her body. Thrusting her feet into a pair of casual loafers made of dark blue denim, she was ready.

Walking into the hall, she saw her mother in front of the TV, watching some *saas-bahu* serial. "Mom, I won't be home for dinner," she said, leaning down to kiss Ambika on her cheek.

"Oh! Who are you going out with?" asked the mother, eyeing her daughter's casual clothes with a small scowl drawing her eyebrows together. Ambika was confident that Shreya was not meeting some boyfriend, not dressed the way she was, in torn jeans of all clothes.

"Just some friends," said Shreya, not meeting her mother's eyes as she walked towards the front door.

"When will you be back? This is not Durban, you understand? Delhi isn't the safest place for single women, especially young and beautiful ones."

"Thanks for the warning, Mom. I'll make sure someone drops me home. Bye." She stepped out and shut the door firmly before her mother could stop her with further questions and suggestions. Taking the elevator down from the tenth floor where they lived, she walked out of the compound, feeling so free and happy as she looked forward to spending the evening with her newfound friend. She was used to leading an independent life back in Durban and the past couple of weeks from the time they had arrived in Delhi had been anything but that; what with the rounds of visiting relatives and friends—all complete strangers to Shreya. But her mother had been insistent, and Shreya didn't really have the heart to quarrel with her. Today was the first time she was going out on her own. Phew!

Saket Metro Station was not very far from the service apartment the Udhas family was staying in and Shreya decided to walk there. Once inside, she studied the map to find out how to get to Barakhamba Metro Station before purchasing a token. Getting into the train at the yellow line, she waited for eleven stations to pass before stepping out at Rajiv Chowk and catching the blue line. While the stations were crowded, it was all pretty orderly and Shreya had no difficulty navigating her way through the escalators and platforms to catch the train and managed to get out a few minutes later at the next station.

Her phone pinged just when she was stepping out of the train. "Where are you?"

"Getting off the metro at Barakhamba."

"Sending you the location to my office," read the next message before Chirag did exactly that.

"Gotcha! See you soon." She exited the station to walk towards his office building which was barely five minutes away. Her lips stretched in a wide smile when she saw Chirag stepping out of the elevator to greet her at the building's reception.

"Hey, good to see you," he said, giving her a hug. "And you look cute."

Shreya couldn't do much about the colour which rose up her cheeks as she gazed into his face, the five o'clock shadow only adding to his handsome looks. "Good to see you too. How was your day?"

"Productive," he said, taking her elbow in his to guide her towards the lift.

"You aren't done yet?" she asked.

"Half an hour to go," he grimaced. "Hope you don't mind."

"Not at all. Do I get a grand tour of your office?" she asked as they got into the lift.

Pressing the button to the fifth floor, he said, "Why not?"

"How big is your agency?" she asked, curious to know. In fact, she wanted to know everything about him.

"Come and see for yourself," he invited when they stepped out into the lobby. Pointing a finger towards a pair of wide glass doors, he said, "There it is."

"Chibha Advertising Agency," she read the board.

"Yep. Chibha stands for Chirag Bhatia."

"That's cute," she said, smiling at him.

"Coffee or tea?" he asked as they stepped inside the plush office space which took up half of the building floor.

"Coffee, I think. How many people work for you?" she asked, stunned to see the large room divided into multiple bays.

"Sixty-two at the last count, not including yours truly."

"Really!" Shreya stopped in her tracks to look at him, thoroughly impressed. "That's a big operation."

"It is," he said, smiling as he pulled her along with him to the furthermost cabin, which was the biggest of the five cabins in the office, and belonged to the CEO and Managing Director.

"I am impressed," she declared, giving him a wide smile.

"You should be," he said, winking. Lifting the intercom, he asked for two coffees. "Why don't you sit down? I just need to get the last bit of stuff out of the way.

"Sure." But instead of settling down, she circled around his office, checking out the pen-and-ink sketches on one wall. They not only looked aesthetic, but were well-detailed. She stepped closer to see if there was a signature, her eyes going wide when she saw the initials CB penned at the right lower corner of every sketch.

Whew!

The adjacent wall had a batch of framed certificates which claimed how highly educated and professionally trained Chirag Bhatia was, from both Delhi University and the Miami Ad School in Florida, in the US of A. The third wall, behind Chirag's desk, was a sheet of glass which looked over the garden at the back.

"Come and have your coffee," called Chirag, turning to look at his guest, his gaze admiring as he studied her slender figure, the denim material taut over her bottom which appeared neatly rounded and sexy to boot.

She turned around to walk towards him, not missing the way his hair appeared in peaks, as if he had been running his hand through it. Hadn't it been neatly combed back when he went down to meet her? "Is there a problem?" she asked him, pointing a finger at his laptop as she went to sit in front of his desk.

He frowned as he sipped from his coffee mug. "Kind of. The darn campaign isn't falling in place. My team was confident that we had everything together, but," he shook his head, "the end result is no good."

"What is it for?" she asked, sipping from her mug. "Mmm, this is damn good."

He smiled. "Isn't it? It's instant, but not machine made."

"Aah! No wonder. So tell me about your campaign."

"It's for a new fashion house which caters to both men and women."

"Do you have an age range?" she asked, not bothered about interrupting him.

"Fifteen to thirty-five."

"May I take a look?" She placed her empty coffee mug on the table before walking towards where he was sitting behind his desk.

"Feel free." He turned the laptop to face her.

Standing at his side, she scrolled through the slides, checking them one by one, her focus completely on what she was doing.

As for Chirag, he took a deep whiff of the scent of roses wafting from her, along with something unique, all Shreya. He didn't know if she was conscious of her left arm pressing against his right. But he was only too aware of their nearness and found himself affected by it. He eyed her profile, taking in the softness of her cheek and the shape of her shell-like ear, the yellow hoop moving to and fro as she scrolled the mouse with her left hand.

Conscious of his gaze, Shreya turned around to glance at him, meeting his dark gaze boldly. "What?" she asked, startled to find his mouth so close to her own. She would have to lean barely a couple of inches to kiss him. Taking a deep breath to quell the temptation, she lifted an eyebrow at him.

"Are you able to see what's wrong?" he asked her about the campaign, without batting an eyelid.

"I think so. The clothes are too young for the models who appear way too confident… you know, kind of jaded for something so funky; I would even say quirky. You need fresh faces. I know you mentioned the upper age limit as thirty-five, but still, it would be best if you used teenage models. Twenty, at the most."

"Will you consider yourself a suitable model for this campaign?" he asked, lowering his gaze to eye her clothes.

She shrugged. "Maybe clothes wise. But not age wise. You will need much younger people."

He turned around to run through the slides on his laptop from the beginning till the end, keeping her feedback in mind. "You are right." He got up suddenly, feeling recharged now that he understood the issue which had been bothering him. "Thanks, Shreya," he said, giving her a hug.

She grinned at him. "No problemo."

"Five more minutes, I promise," he said, "and we can leave."

"Sure."

"If you'll wait here, I'll be back soon." He left his cabin to go and speak to his campaign manager, and returned in five minutes as promised. "Shall we leave?"

"I'm ready," said Shreya, stretching lazily as she got up from the visitor's chair she had been ensconced in.

Chirag felt saliva pooling in his mouth when he noticed the way her supple body stretched when she lifted her arms above her head, drawing his gaze to her lush breasts. For such a slim woman, she was well endowed. And her top separated itself from the waistband of her jeans, exposing her flat midriff and her navel button, making him go breathless for a couple of moments. Not saying anything, he went to pick the dark grey canvas jacket from the back of his chair before slipping it on. Leaving the buttons open, he was ready to go. "Drinks, you said."

"Yes. Beer?" she turned to look at him in enquiry as they stepped into the elevator.

"Beer, it is."

"Before we go, I want to make something clear."

"What?" he asked, looking at her in curiosity. She fascinated him, this Shreya Udhas from South Africa.

"We will go Dutch."

"Eh?" he frowned. The condition she laid down was completely novel to him. Every single woman he had dated so far, had always expected him to pay for everything, including the expensive trinkets they seemed to crave. All because he was a rich businessman from an even richer family.

"You heard me."

"Have it your way," he said, "this time," he added, his voice barely a whisper.

She laughed. "I heard you."

They walked to the car park, to where his brilliant blue Audi was parked at the place allotted for the CEO of Chibha. Unlocking it with electronic keys, he opened the passenger door, waiting for her to settle in before walking to the driver's seat.

"This is superb," she said, stroking her hand over the cream-coloured buttery leather of the seat.

"I'm glad you like it," he said, reversing out of the car park.

"Where are we going?" she asked.

"My Bar Headquarters is the name of the place. It's not far from here."

They continued to chat as he drove out of the
compound and on to the road. It wasn't long before
they reached the bar. Chirag stopped at the entrance
before handing the key to a valet. Taking her elbow in his
hand, he escorted her inside the barn-like structure with
a high ceiling. Seeing that it was well-crowded, they still
managed to get a corner table, all because Chirag knew
the owner and had called him in advance.

"This is nice," declared Shreya, turning left and
right to take in the ambience. There was music coming
from hidden speakers and while it was loud, it was still
possible to hold a conversation.

"Glad you like it. They have DJ music after nine pm
and even make space for dancing."

"Sounds good," she smiled, sitting down in the chair
he pulled out for her.

Seating himself opposite to her, he said, "We'll come
dancing in the weekend if you're free."

"I'd love to," she responded, before studying the bar
menu a waiter handed her.

"They have a pint bucket. What's your preference?"
he asked, checking out the list.

"Budweiser?" she asked, lifting her gaze from the menu to look up at him.

"Works for me. A small snack? The *chicken pakoda* is good," he recommended.

She bit her forefinger, looking up at him from under her eyelashes. "I'm vegetarian," she said.

He looked up from the menu, a surprised expression on his face. "You are? Shreya from South Africa?"

A small smile lit up her face. "Hehe! My whole family, yes."

"Have you never been tempted to try something non-vegetarian?" he asked, curious to know. He couldn't imagine someone not wanting to eat chicken or mutton.

She shook her head from side to side. "Probably the way I've been brought up," she shrugged, "I've never been tempted. Not even eggs."

"Ouch! Okay. So…"

She lifted a hand in front of her. "You please go ahead and have whatever you want. It won't affect me. I promise not to grimace," she said, giving him a broad wink.

He laughed softly, staring at her beautiful face. "Let me go vegetarian for today." Checking out the food menu again, he suggested, "Nachos?"

"Sounds good."

"Then that's what we'll have."

"I'm sorry I…"

He reached over to take her hand in his. "Don't be," he said, cutting off her apology midway. Chirag placed their order with the waiter before giving her his complete attention. "So, how's life in Durban? Have you been living there long?"

"Forever," she said, answering his second question first. "I was born there. I love my life, with loads of friends living close by."

"You teach yoga, right? How did you get into yoga?"

"Is it twenty questions time?" she asked, her eyes laughing at him.

He grinned at her. "Call it whatever you want. How else do I get to know all about you?"

"Is that what you want to do? Know all about me?" she asked, continuing to tease him.

"Every damn thing, yes," he declared, nodding to the waiter who had brought their beer—five one-pint bottles half-buried in a bucket of ice. He gave a nod when the waiter offered to open two bottles, taking the first one from the man and handing it over to Shreya. Once the waiter left, Chirag lifted his bottle to her in a toast, "To getting to know you well."

"To knowing every damn thing about you too," she said, grinning at him as she lifted her bottle to touch its tip to his.

That had gone well, him declaring his immediate intention. It had also given her a chance to declare her intention of getting to know him. Good!

"I am the eldest child of Sunil and Ambika Udhas and was born twenty-two years ago," she drawled exaggeratedly, as if she was telling a story. She stopped to tell him, "I'll understand if you yawned."

He burst out laughing. "Not so far. Go on."

"You already know I have three siblings, all younger to me."

"Hmm mmm."

"Now about you," she invited, drinking from her bottle.

"Youngest of three, born to Deven and Chandrika Bhatia. My sisters, Dipali and Chaaya, are both married."

"Do they live here in Delhi?" she asked.

"Nope. Dipali lives in Washington and Chaaya is in Dubai."

"Are you an uncle yet?" she asked, curious to know if he liked children.

"Not quite yet. Dipali is expecting her first baby in three months or so."

"And you? When do you plan to get married?" She slipped in the question, wondering if he would answer.

"Me? Marriage? Not for a few years yet."

"Have you met Ms Right yet?"

"If I have, I wouldn't be out on a date with you." He turned to the waiter and nodded when the man asked if he should serve them.

His last sentence impressed Shreya more than anything else. "One man woman, are you?" she asked, lifting a shapely eyebrow in query.

He shrugged. "Yet to find out," he said, giving her a wink. "What about you? Do you have a boyfriend back home in Durban?"

"I wish. If that were the case, I wouldn't be here on a bridegroom hunt along with my parents."

"Are you?" he asked, popping a piece of nachos into his mouth, and munching on it.

"Am I what?"

"On the hunt for a bridegroom?"

She grimaced, shaking her head. "No."

"Then?"

She sighed. "My mother is determined to get me married off to someone rich and handsome—in that order—from India, preferably Delhi."

"What about your father?"

"My poor dad is here on business for two months. Mom took this opportunity to bring all of us here, planning the hunt for a bridegroom during the trip."

"Must be tough, I suppose."

"It is."

"Didn't you protest when she suggested the idea to you?"

"Suggested? Huh!" Shreya rolled her eyes. "My mother doesn't know the meaning of the word. She simply bulldozed me into her plans."

"So, what happens if something clicks? If your mother manages to find the right man for you?"

"I'm expecting to have the last word."

"Won't she twist your arm?"

"Nope."

"Why agree to this charade in the first place? If I understand it correctly, that's what it is, no? A charade?"

She grimaced. "It was simpler to fall in with her wishes. For one thing, I liked the idea of visiting Delhi after ten years. We all did, in fact. If the only way to come here was to include a groom hunt, then so be it," she shrugged.

Smart woman! Chirag was impressed by the way she had grabbed the opportunity to get what she wanted — time to spend in Delhi. "What about your job?"

"I haven't taken leave in the two-plus years I've been working there. They didn't mind me taking a couple of months off. What about you? Do you take time off? Or are you a workaholic?"

"I love my work and do spend all kinds of hours doing it. But I also have fun away from it."

"What do you do when you are not the CEO of Chibha? Do you party a lot? Like the one at Nishaan's place?"

"Party, yes, sometimes. But I do spend quiet evenings with friends. Like what we are doing now. While I don't mind crowds, I prefer to be with a few people most of the time."

"Any hobbies?"

"I swim…"

Her eyes lit up. "You do? I love to swim too."

"What say we go swimming at my club on Saturday? You can even bring your brothers and sister if you want. I'm sure they will enjoy it. I'll call a few friends of mine too."

"That sounds lovely."

"It's a date, then. Do you want to drink some more? Or shall we go on to Chandni Chowk?" he asked, noticing her placing her empty bottle back in the bucket.

"Ready for some street food," she said, closing her mouth when a burp overtook her. "Sorry about that."

He laughed. "You don't need to apologise so often," he said, getting up to take her hand in his, once he placed the cash for their bill on the table.

"Let me give you my share," she said, pulling the zip on her sling bag.

"Later! You pay for the food, okay?"

"Are you sure?" She turned her face up to his.

"Absolutely, yes," he said. Unable to resist her, he leaned forward to kiss the tip of her nose.

She squinted, trying to gaze at the tip of her nose, wondering why he had kissed her there.

He laughed, watching her antics as she pressed her forefinger under her nose to push it up, as if it would give her a better view. "Shall we go?"

She stopped her efforts immediately to give him a nod. "Let's."

They stepped out of My Bar Headquarters and Chirag lifted a hand to someone. In the meanwhile, the valet brought his car around to the front. Handing the car key to the driver-on-hire, Chirag instructed him, "Listen, Soman, you can drop us outside Chandni Chowk and then leave the car at my house. Hand over the keys to my watchman, okay?"

"Yes sir," said Soman, taking the car outside.

"What all do you get to eat in Chandni Chowk?" asked Shreya, smacking her lips in anticipation. She had eaten barely two pieces of the nachos Chirag had ordered at the bar.

"While they are famous for their *parantha*, *naan* and *bhatura*, you will truly flip for the *kachori*, *aloo tikki*, *papdi chaat* and the like. As for the local sweets, the *jalebis* are to die for."

"Stop! Please stop! Unless you want me to flood your car with my saliva," protested Shreya, placing a restraining hand over his mouth.

He laughed at her words, holding her hand against his mouth as he kissed her fingers in turn.

Suddenly becoming aware that there was a driver in the front seat, Shreya tried to withdraw her hand, only he refused to let go.

Moving her hand away from his mouth, Chirag placed it on his thigh and held it in place, not at all keen to let go of her.

Reluctant to make a fuss, she let her hand rest on his leg, only to become conscious of the hard muscles, making her want to run her hand along the length of his thigh. She curled her hand under his, making an effort to stop herself as she turned away from him to look out of the window.

Feeling the restlessness in her hand, he curled his fingers around hers, stroking his thumb slowly and rhythmically over her palm, pausing every time he felt the racing pulse at her wrist.

A deep sigh of longing shuddered through Shreya's being, as she felt a sudden desire to be held close to his hard frame.

"Shrey…" Her name was a soft whisper as Chirag turned his face leftwards, keen to have her attention back on him.

"What?" She turned around jerkily to face him, once again.

"Not to forget the *lassi* they serve in *kulhads*…"

Her breath coming out in a whoosh, Shreya felt a deep sense of relief at his teasing; as the heated atmosphere in the car had become kind of difficult to bear. "Are you a glutton?" she asked, her honey brown eyes alight with amusement.

"Eh?" He gave her a mock glare as he patted his flat abdomen. "Do I seem like one?"

Her eyes drawn to his stomach, she smiled. "I suppose not," she admitted. "But you love food."

Running his eyes over her slender body, his gaze stopping to take stock of her twin mounds, he clenched his hands as he felt a powerful urge to hold them. Finally, lifting his gaze to meet hers, he asked, "Don't you? And I can't see any spare flesh on you either."

Soft colour ran over Shreya's cheeks as she met the heat in his black eyes boldly, her tongue coming out to trace the shape of her lips suddenly gone dry.

"Don't do that. Unless you want me to do something drastic," he said, staring at her damp lips.

"Like what?" she asked, leaning closer to him.

"We have company," he warned, drawing her head to his shoulder, and holding it there, even as he turned to stare at the traffic out of the front window.

"What would you have done if we had no company?" she asked in a whisper, turning her head on his shoulder to speak into his ear, feeling thrilled when she felt her lips brushing against his wavy hair.

"Behave!" he ordered.

"I don't believe it."

"Eh?" He pushed her away to sit up straight. "What don't you believe?"

"That you will behave if we had no company," she said, straight faced.

He burst out laughing on hearing her words. "I have a good mind to cancel our dinner plans and take you to my apartment."

"Oh no, please!" she begged dramatically, fluttering her eyelashes at him. "I can become damn cranky if I get no food."

"Cat!" he accused, leaning far away from her to cross his arms over his massive chest as he eyed her. Too damn charming, that's what she was!

"Do you have one?" she asked, sitting up straight.

"Two, actually. Jack and Jill are both strays I took in when they were babies."

"How old are they now?"

"About two years."

"Can I see them?" she asked, her eyes glowing with excitement.

"You will need to get past my parents to meet them," he warned, his eyes dancing with amusement.

She placed a finger on her chin, thinking hard. "Are your parents keen to get you married?" she asked, coming directly to the point.

"Aren't all Indian parents?" he asked her right back.

"Chirag, be serious. Do your parents want to marry you off urgently?"

"Not urgently, no." He had made them promise they wouldn't bother him regarding his marriage, not until he turned thirty-two. And that was still four more years to go.

"What does that even mean?" she asked, giving him an irritated glance as the driver slowed the car to a stop.

"We will need to get down from your side," he said, reaching across to open her door.

Shreya got out to stand on the footpath, waiting for his answer as she watched him slide out of the car before standing next to her. How tall was he? Right now, he seemed to tower over her.

"We need to go that way," he said, pointing to the busy lane further to their left.

"Okay. But you still haven't answered my question," she grumbled, falling into step beside him, glad that he was holding her hand firmly. *Or I might become lost in this crowd of pedestrians and push carts,* she thought, turning left and right as she took in her surroundings. People spoke loudly, obviously trying to hear above the din, even as many of them went in and out of shop entrances on both sides.

"The *khau galli* is through there," he said, pointing to their right.

She removed her phone from her sling bag. "Take some pictures?" she asked, unlocking it before offering it to him.

Chirag couldn't believe his eyes when she turned around to walk backwards, obviously expecting him to click pictures of her. Shaking his head in amusement, he did just that, clicking away as he continued to walk forward. He planned to send all those pictures to his phone before handing hers back to Shreya.

"You still haven't told me what your parents' intentions are. Don't you want me to meet your Jack and Jill?" she asked, scowling up at him once she had enough pictures. "How about a selfie?" she continued, before he could respond.

Giving her an amazed glance, he took his phone out to take selfies from different angles, covering both ends of the lane as well as many of the shop fronts.

"Is it always like this? So busy? Or is it because it's evening?"

"A bit less during the day, maybe. But always busy," he said, taking her elbow to turn her left again.

"How far?" she asked.

"Another minute," he responded patiently. "And as for your other question, my parents won't push me into marriage in a hurry. They are ready to wait."

"Phew! That's a relief. When can we go meet your cats?"

"Do you like cats?" he asked, not missing the fact how insistent she was.

"Adore them."

"We'll go soon," he promised, before sweeping his arm over the *khau galli* in front of them. "Here you go, this is *the place* for Delhi street food."

She stood right where she was, taking a deep whiff of the myriad aromas wafting from the many eateries. Many of them had a counter right at the front, where men were making *naans* over open fires or frying *bhature* in extra-large frying pans. There were tables and benches behind where customers could sit. These were packed to the hilt, though people kept coming and going.

"Let's go a bit further, shall we?" Chirag walked forward, continuing to hold her hand.

"Of course." She looked to the right and to the left, taking in the atmosphere even as she clicked more pictures. She even insisted that he pose for some of them.

"*Aloo tikki?*" he asked, stopping at a shop to their right.

"Oh yes, please," she said, excited to see a huge iron skillet where a man was turning around dozens of *tikkis* as customers waited their turn.

"Hey, these have *channa* inside them," squealed Shreya, munching on hers sometime later. "My cook makes it purely from potatoes."

"This is special to Delhi," he said, more interested in watching her eat than having his own. They were sharing a plate of two *tikkis* as they were eager to taste as many of the items as possible.

Noticing that he wasn't eating, she offered her own *tikki* to him. "Go on, take a bite. It's damn good."

Holding her slender wrist firmly in his large hand, he took a bite from her snack, not taking his eyes off hers. "You're right, it tastes too delicious," he declared, opening his mouth to take the rest of the *tikki* into it, deliberately running the tip of his tongue over her fingers.

"I'm going to eat yours," she declared in a choked voice, looking down at the plate in her hand instead of into his heated gaze. Her mind running a mile a minute, she focused on the food from then on, not too sure of where Chirag's flirting would lead them. She supposed she couldn't blame him completely, as she found herself giving back almost as much as she got.

And there was the fact that she had as good as invited herself to his home. Not that he had agreed to her suggestion, at least, not yet.

They took their time sampling the wares from many counters, walking leisurely around, with Shreya taking hundreds of pictures.

"Are you on Instagram?" he asked suddenly.

"Yes," she smiled.

"Aah!" Now he knew why she was constantly on her phone camera. "Do you want anything else?" he asked, once they finished drinking *lassi*.

She shook her head, patting her stomach. "Can't." When he reached for his wallet, she placed a hand on his arm. "You paid for the drinks. Now let me."

He stared at her for a few moments, as if unsure of how to deal with her offer before giving her a small nod. "Okay." Once she paid off their bill, he took her hand before turning around to trace their way back out of Chandni Chowk. "Shall we walk for a bit? Or do you have a curfew?"

"No curfew, we can walk."

And they did for more than an hour, going wherever their feet took them. They didn't speak much as they were both deep in thought, each wondering where this new relationship was taking them.

It was past midnight when Chirag dropped Shreya outside her building, making the cab wait for him. "Goodnight, Shrey," he said, stepping out to open the gate for her.

"Goodnight, Chirag. And thank you. I had a lovely time."

"So did I. And thanks for the help at work."

She waved him off. "Hey, that was nothing."

"Dinner at my home tomorrow?" The words slipped out of Chirag's mouth of their own volition. He suddenly realised he was reluctant to part company with her.

"With your cats?" Her eyes lit up with enthusiasm.

He rolled his eyes. "That wasn't exactly what I meant. But yes, you can meet Jack and Jill. I had better go before you say something else to make me feel lesser than a cat," he grumbled playfully.

She laughed softly, shaking her head. Going on the tips of her toes, she held his face between her palms before pressing her mouth to the deep cleft in his chin, her nerves sizzling when she felt the day-old bristles scraping her lips. "I want to meet them only because they are your cats, okay?"

His hands spanning her waist, he pulled her closer to his body. "Is that supposed to make me feel better?" he asked, kissing her cheek.

"You mean it didn't?" she asked, her eyes going wide as she pretended to be surprised.

"Nope." He kissed a corner of her lips.

"I need to go."

"Just a moment," he said, burying his face in the crook of her neck, breathing deeply to bring some kind of control over his clamouring body. He took several moments before letting her go. "See you tomorrow."

"Bye." Shreya held the gate post firmly. It was a while before her knees stopped shaking.

5

Shreya let herself into the silent apartment, glad to note that none of her family members was awake. She tiptoed her way to the bedroom she shared with her sister. She took the nightshirt which lay folded at the foot of her bed and went to the attached bathroom to change, not keen to disturb the sleeping Aadhira.

She discarded her jeans and top before having a quick wash and donning her nightshirt, her mind running over the evening spent with Chirag. It had been fun and she had enjoyed his company. She touched her lips, still feeling the imprint of his firm and bristled chin, even as she wondered how his lips would have felt; the thin upper one and the sensually thick lower one. A small shiver danced down her spine as her imagination overran with images of kissing Chirag. Taking a deep breath, she shook them off while continuing to ponder about him.

He was a smart businessman it seemed. And it had been exciting finding a solution to the problem he had been facing with one of his projects. With a smile on her face, she went to lie on her single bed, unable to stop thinking of the handsome and intelligent Chirag. She had found out that his birthday fell on December 19, which made him a Sagittarius. She took the phone from the bedside table and did a quick search on the internet, to find out the qualities of that particular star sign.

Checking out a couple of websites, she quickly read through the highlights, shutting her phone with a smile on her face. One phrase stood out above all else—noncommittal—and she liked that. It meant he wasn't going to jump into proposing marriage. Right now, despite all her mother's efforts, Shreya was clear that she wasn't going to marry anytime soon. Instead of picking up a quarrel with Ambika, she had decided to go along with her plans, intending to put a stop if anything seemed on the verge of clicking. It was a good thing Nishaan Ahuja was in love with some other woman, and Shreya had had a lucky escape. If she knew her mother, it wouldn't be long before Ambika found another suitable match for her eldest born. But until then, Shreya intended to have fun with her new friend.

She was looking forward to dinner at Chirag's home, meeting his cats. Okay, she will meet his parents too. But well, as long as both she and Chirag were sure nothing was going to come out of it. And not a word to her own mother, or Ambika might set out to find all about Chirag Bhatia and his family, and plan a match for her daughter.

Shreya grinned to herself, closing her eyes as she willed sleep to come. This Delhi trip might turn out to be entertaining, it seemed.

Chirag got into the cab and gave the driver the address to his bungalow, settling back to gaze out of the window. He had heard his phone ping multiple times, but wasn't keen to check the messages, his mind on Shreya Udhas.

For one thing, she was beautiful. For another, she was exceptionally bright. The way she had solved the problem with his ad project had been nothing short of brilliant. And so swiftly too. As for her slim, but luscious figure, she was totally drool-worthy. It had been a lot of effort for Chirag not to simply throw her over his shoulder and carry her to his bachelor pad in Janakpuri. That's how much he was tempted.

But it was obvious that Shreya was a complete innocent. It stood out a mile; actually. As of now, Chirag was only looking for a short-term affair. And he wasn't sure if she would be open to that. But he still wanted to spend time with her, as her intelligent mind was even more fascinating than her sexy body.

If some other woman had chased him about meeting his cats, Chirag might have believed that they were using Jack and Jill as an excuse to pursue him. But with Shreya, it had been only too obvious that she was keen to meet his pets. He smiled to himself when he thought of the way she had pranced about Chandni Chowk, posing for pictures as well as clicking many. She was still an enthusiastic child in the body of a young woman. And he was enamoured, yes!

He had found out that her birthday fell on February 2, which made her an Aquarius. He had read somewhere long ago that the women under this star sign tended to be rebellious in nature. Was she, really? Here she was, falling in with her mother's plan to find her a bridegroom, even if she personally wasn't interested in getting married.

Chirag sat up straight when it suddenly hit him. Shreya had fallen in with her mother's plans, which showed her affection for her parent. But what he had gleaned from their conversations was this: that it was an opportunity to holiday in Delhi. And Shreya had no plans of actually marrying anyone. Oh yes, Aquarian women could be stubborn too.

Right now, that was good news to him. Now, all he had to do was find out if she would be interested in having a brief fling with him.

Yes!

"Hey, Mom, good morning!" Chirag raced down the staircase of his bungalow the next morning, with Jack perched on his right shoulder while Jill lay in his cradled arms.

"Good morning, Chirag. Did you sleep well?" asked Chandrika Bhatia, smiling at her handsome and strapping son.

"You came pretty late, I think." Deven lifted his face from where it had been buried in the newspaper, to ask Chirag.

"That's right, Dad. I went out for dinner with a friend." He let the cats down on the sofa before pouring himself a mug of coffee from the flask on the centre table. "What's for breakfast?"

"There's egg omelette and *aloo paratha*. Unless you want something else," said his mother.

"Omelette is good. Let me ask Ramu *kaka* to toast some bread for me. Oh, by the way, I have invited a friend for dinner. I hope you guys are going to be home this evening."

"Would it be the same friend you had dinner with last evening?" asked Deven, folding the newspaper away to concentrate on his only son.

"We aren't going anywhere," said Chandrika. "Who is this friend? Someone I know?"

Chirag shrugged. "Not sure. Shreya Udhas was there at the party at Nishaan's home the other day…"

"Wait! Are you talking about the Udhas family from Durban?" asked Chandrika. "I met Sunil and Ambika Udhas at the party. They were talking about an alliance for their daughter with Nishaan." She couldn't help wondering if this Shreya Udhas was the same girl.

"Your memory is astounding, Mom," said Chirag, hugging his mother. "That's the family. They were meeting Nishaan for Shreya's alliance. Only, Nishaan already has a girlfriend. So, that didn't work."

"I didn't see the girl though," said Chandrika.

"Exactly what I was thinking," said Deven. "Is this same girl your friend who is coming over for dinner?"

"Yes, the very same."

"Er… does that mean…?"

Chirag lifted his hand to stop his mother from speaking further. "I know what you are going to ask, Mom. But no. Shreya is just a friend. She loves cats and is coming over to meet Jack and Jill." He shut his mind up when it gently reminded him of his body's reaction to the so-called friend the earlier evening. He had taken a long, cold shower before going to bed, only to stay awake half the night, thinking of the beautiful Shreya.

Tch! Chandrika couldn't help but feel a wave of disappointment. For a minute there, she had felt thrilled that Chirag was bringing home a young woman for dinner. Well, he insisted that he needed at least four more years before thinking of marriage. But a mother could hope, right?

Chirag went to the kitchen to request the cook for his omelette and bread toast before returning to the living room. "Oh, another thing. Can we have a vegetarian meal for tonight? Shreya does not eat non-veg."

"Not even eggs?" asked Deven, his eyes twinkling with mirth. He had been quietly studying the fleeting emotions on his son's face—the ones Chirag had been trying hard to control—and had rightly concluded that this Shreya was not just a friend as his son claimed.

"Nope." Whistling to the cats, Chirag threw a cloth ball across the room and laughed when they went gambolling after it.

"Alright. Will there be a problem if I make one chicken dish?" asked Chandrika.

"That shouldn't be an issue."

"He would know, wouldn't he? They went out for dinner last night," muttered Deven on an aside to his wife, when Chirag went to get his breakfast tray from the kitchen. It was still early for his parents to have their first meal as it was barely 8.30 am. But he needed to get to work.

Chandrika gave her husband a broad smile. "I know."

Chirag fed pieces of omelette to the cats which gobbled the pieces quickly, begging for more.

"They are too fat," protested Chandrika, "and have already eaten a boiled egg each in the morning."

"Huh?" Chirag looked down at Jack and Jill who were both eyeing his plate greedily. "No more, guys. Or Grandma says, 'no lunch'."

They turned around to gaze at Chandrika, as if they clearly understood what Chirag was saying.

"That's right. No lunch if you eat more of your dad's breakfast," said Chandrika firmly, her black eyes twinkling with laughter. In the beginning, Chandrika had protested long and hard when Chirag had brought the two kittens home, grumbling that it would be left to her to take care of them. But barely a couple of weeks later, she had become the kittens' biggest fan, spending a lot of time playing with them. The best part was when Chandrika realised that it didn't need a lot of work to manage cats. They were pretty independent and did not need to be taken on walks. With their bungalow set in the middle of a spacious garden, the kittens lived a completely independent life. All Chandrika needed to do was ensure they were fed regularly, that too, with the help of a cook and two maids.

"Are you on leave, Dad?" asked Chirag, keeping his empty breakfast plate aside, laughing when he saw the cats searching for any leftover titbits, only to be disappointed.

Deven worked for a private bank as a financial consultant and had been disappointed in the beginning when his only son had insisted on starting his own business. Worried, more like. After seeing Chirag's success, the father had accepted that his son had been right. He smiled at Chirag's question now. "That's right. Your mother and I are going to a movie with some friends."

Chirag whistled softly. His workaholic father seemed to be taking life easy for a change. "That's awesome, Dad. Dinner…?"

Deven lifted a hand to stop Chirag from speaking further. "No worries. The show is at 11 am, and we should be home by early evening at the most."

"Right. I'll take myself off then. Have a meeting at 9.30," said Chirag, going up the stairs to his room, chuckling when both Jack and Jill followed him.

6

Shreya went down to lie on the marble floor next to the sleeping cats, completely enamoured. It didn't even strike the spontaneous Aquarian that she was in Chirag's home for the first time; will be meeting his parents, also for the first time. She reached with the tip of her left forefinger and gently rubbed it over the top of the white cat's head—with little bits of black markings on her forehead, paws, and black rings on her white tail. She was lying on top of the black cat—with a white snout, under belly, and socks. "You're so cute, both of you," said Shreya, in a gentle whisper, not keen to wake them up.

Jill opened her eyes in a slit to check out the stranger, stretching her fore paws lazily, and managing to wake up Jack who slipped from under her to walk over to Shreya, pressing his nose to her head as he sniffed her.

"They are awake," squealed Shreya, turning to look at Chirag, as if it was an incredible achievement, for both the cats and herself. She got up to sit, laughing when the cats jumped into her lap in turn, purring loudly. "They are so friendly. This is Jack, right?" she asked Chirag as she ran her hand down the black fur, from his neck to his tail.

"That's right." It had been barely ten minutes since she arrived and she was already completely focused on the cats, which left Chirag rather miffed. He stared at her now, as she lay sprawled on the floor, her fitted pastel pink cotton pants clinging to her shapely bottom. Her short white top had ridden up, giving him a glimpse of her bare waist. She appeared damn sexy! And he wanted her in his arms.

Completely unaware of Chirag's gaze on her, she continued to admire his cats. "And this is Jill." Shreya was in cat heaven as she stroked Jill's white tail, admiring the black rings at even intervals. "So cute!" she said once again as she ran her hands over the two of them.

Desperate to distract himself, Chirag quickly took pictures from his phone camera, recording the cute scene of Shreya and his cats to posterity. Once done, he asked, "Will you have a drink? Juice or beer?"

She turned around to glance at him, half her attention still on the cats. "What do you plan to have?" she asked.

"Whisky and soda." That was the only drink which might help calm down his libido. And Chirag had just discovered something new about himself. He was jealous of his cats!

"I'll have the same. Thanks." And she went right back to playing with Jack and Jill, throwing the cloth ball which Chirag had handed her. Her spontaneous laughter rang out in the spacious hall when she saw the way they raced across the hallway on all their fours before fighting over the ball.

Chandrika stepped down the staircase and walked towards her son's guest, drawn by the tinkling laughter. "Oh, you found the cats. Hello, I'm Chandrika, Chirag's mother. And I guess you are Shreya Udhas."

Shreya drew her gaze away from the cats reluctantly to glance at Chirag's mother, getting up gracefully to stand in front of the older woman. "Hello, Aunty, nice to meet you," she said, shaking Chandrika's hand with a smile.

Chandrika studied their dinner guest blatantly, liking what she saw. She was sure the younger woman would be a good candidate for the role of her daughter-in-law. If only Chirag was so inclined. But she dared not make the suggestion to her son, not if she didn't want her head bitten off. Chirag was fixated about his career, his focus completely on his ad agency. Any suggestion of finding him a life partner would be vetoed mercilessly.

"Chirag says you live in Durban?"

"That's right, Aunty. You have a beautiful home," complimented Shreya. And she meant it, at least what she had seen of their bungalow so far. The hall was large, with multiple cosy corners where comfortable sofas were grouped together. The glass showcase against one wall displayed figurines of glass and ceramic from around the world. Someone obviously travelled a lot in the Bhatias' household.

"Thank you, dear. Let me ask Chirag to show you around." Turning towards the staircase when she heard the sound of footsteps, Chandrika said, "This is Chirag's father."

"Hello Uncle!" greeted Shreya, smiling at an older version of Chirag, who stepped down into the hall to stand in front of her.

"Hello, Shreya, welcome to our home. Have you met Jack and Jill?" asked Deven, a twinkle in his dark eyes.

Shreya's smile became wider as she nodded vigorously. "Oh yes, Uncle. They are so cute," she said, turning around to watch the gambolling cats as they still fought over the cloth ball.

"Here you go, your drink." Chirag handed her a glass of whisky and soda packed with ice cubes. Turning to his parents, he asked, "What do you guys want to have?"

"Whisky for me," said Deven, "on the rocks."

"I'll have vodka with orange," said Chandrika. Turning to their guest, she said, "Will you excuse me for a moment? Let me ask Ramu to serve the snacks," before walking towards the back of the house where the kitchen was.

"Come, my dear," invited Deven, leading her towards one corner of the hall before pointing to a two-seater. "Do sit down and tell me all about yourself."

Placing her glass on a side table, Shreya sat down, sighing with pleasure when she almost sank into the silken upholstery. "I have come down to Delhi with my family for a long holiday of sorts. Otherwise, we live in Durban."

Deven nodded, accepting the glass Chirag handed him before taking a sip. "Perfect!" he said, lifting his glass in a toast to his son before turning his attention to Shreya once again. "Have you been living there for long?"

"Forever! I was born there," smiled Shreya. She stopped speaking when she felt sudden heat invading her body when Chirag settled down right next to her, his thigh brushing against hers. And there was nothing she could do about the hot colour which rose in her cheeks as she gave him a corner-eyed glance, even as she worked hard at keeping her focus on his father. "My grandfather had settled in Durban when my father was still a child."

"Oh, that's interesting. I met your father the other day at the party. Sunil Udhas, right?" Deven continued when Shreya nodded. "He has his own business, he mentioned."

"That's right, Uncle. Even now, Dad is here on work. It is the rest of us who are on holiday."

"Who all would that be?"

Chandrika placed a tray with plates filled with mini spring rolls and samosas accompanied by a variety of chutneys and sauces in front of the sofa Chirag and Shreya were sharing. "You must try these, Shreya. They are all homemade," she suggested.

"Thank you, Aunty. I'd love to," responded Shreya, picking up a mini roll and biting into it. "Mmm… this is so delicious," she declared, after swallowing the piece.

"I'm sure. Shreya is a total foodie," said Chirag, his amused gaze falling on her expressive face.

Before Shreya could respond in kind, she felt the brush of a velvety head against her leg and looked down to see Jack butting his head against her. Laughing, she leaned down to pet him, only for Jill to butt her other leg. "These two are so friendly," she said, laughing in delight.

"More like they want you to feed them whatever is on your plate. Jack and Jill love food too, just like you," teased Chirag.

"Oh! Here I thought they want to be friends with me," responded Shreya, giving him a mock glare before turning her attention back to the cats.

"Please don't feed them, Shreya," insisted Chandrika, "they are already too spoilt as it is."

"Who does the spoiling?" asked Shreya, secretly offering a piece of a samosa's crispy edge, one to each cat.

"I suppose it's all of us," laughed Deven.

"Shrey…" Chirag placed a hand on her arm, giving a small shake of his head when she would have fed more of the samosa to Jack and Jill, who were looking up at her greedily.

"How can I say no, when they ask me so adorably?" Shreya turned her appealing brown gaze to her friend.

Chirag laughed softly before shooing the cats. "Jack, Jill, go away. Ramu *kaka* has prepared chicken for you guys."

Both cats looked up at Chirag as if they understood exactly what he said before racing towards the kitchen, making Shreya laugh some more.

Dinner was a fun affair as she chatted comfortably with the Bhatia parents, while Chirag watched on, his black-as-sin gaze missing nothing. Once they were done, he got up immediately to take Shreya's hand in his. "Come, let's go for a walk."

"Aunty? Do you need help with…?" Shreya stopped mid-sentence when Chandrika waved a hand at her.

"No, no, child. There's no need for that. You go on," said Chandrika, giving their guest an encouraging smile.

Chirag drew her out through a side door and they stepped down into the lawn which was surrounded by trees and flowering bushes. He was glad to finally have her completely to himself.

Stopping in her tracks to take a deep whiff, Shreya's eyes closed of their own accord when she felt the peace stealing over her being. "This is so beautiful."

"I know," agreed Chirag, his eyes watching her intently.

"What?" She looked up at him, raising an eyebrow.

"Beautiful!" he declared before wrapping an arm around her shoulders and pulling her along with him as he walked towards the peripheral of the lawn, under the mango tree at the furthest end where the light was the dimmest. Walking behind it, he leaned against the trunk before pulling her into his arms.

"Chirag?" Shreya looked up at him, her hands splayed on his chest as she wondered what he planned to do. Her breathing hitched when she saw the way he was eyeing her, as a small child would eye a piece of candy.

"Shrey…" He leaned down to press his mouth to her forehead, lifting both his hands to cup her face. He slowly stroked her cheeks with his thumbs, smiling when he felt the heat rising in her face. Breathing deeply of her delightfully feminine scent of roses, he brushed his lips over her eyelids in turn, smiling when he felt the flutter of her eyelashes against his mouth. Tracing a line down her jaw, he pressed his mouth to the pulse beating at her neck, reaching with the tip of his tongue to stroke against it.

Whoosh! Her breath came out in a gasp when she felt his damp tongue over her pulse, making it leap in response, her heart thumping so hard in her rib cage that she thought it might burst out of her chest. She clutched his cotton shirt with both her hands, holding on to him desperately as she felt weakness invade her legs. She gasped some more when he traced the shape of her ear with his tongue, making every single nerve come alive. "Chiraaag…"

"Mmm…" He was relentless in tasting her, as he nibbled his way along her jaw to reach over to the other side and kissing that ear, his arms locked around her slender body.

Shreya turned her head to the side automatically, letting him have his way with her, her mouth tingling with a sudden need to kiss him the way he was kissing her. Lifting her face up towards him, she pressed her mouth to his cheek, her breath hitching when she felt the brush of his five o'clock against her lips, making them tingle some more.

He turned his head to capture her mouth with his, stroking the shape of her lips with his tongue. She tasted so damn delicious!

With a gasp, Shreya opened her mouth to let him slide in his tongue, her head falling back on his shoulder when he explored her mouth thoroughly. She moaned when she felt his large hands cupping her buttocks to pull her closer to his lower body, his hardened manhood throbbing against her abdomen. So! This was how it felt, being plastered against the body of a man! It was a totally new experience to her, and Shreya realised that she liked it. Throwing her arms around his neck, she held on to him tight, going on the tips of her toes which she placed on his large feet, the better to reach him.

It was a long time before they came apart, deep gasps emanating from their throats as they fought for breath. Shreya burrowed her face in his chest while Chirag pressed his cheek to the top of her head. The effort to control his raging libido was humongous, and he fought like a warrior to do exactly that. Finally, when they were breathing normally, he lifted his head to look down at her. "Shrey…"

Shreya raised her face to look up at him, glad for the shadows which hid the heat in her cheeks, or so she believed. Placing her hands on his shoulders, she pushed away from him to stand straight. But she continued to hold on to him as she wasn't sure if her legs wouldn't buckle as they continued to tremble. A soft sigh escaped her lips as she considered the magnitude of her situation. She had been kissed a couple of times before, but those experiences seemed juvenile compared to the heat in Chirag's kisses. She felt her heart flutter as she recalled the passionate kisses they had shared just now. Her mouth tingled in remembrance of the thorough sweep of his tongue over her inner cheeks and palate.

"Does this hurt?" Chirag reached the tip of an index finger to trace her swollen lower lip which was also an angry red.

"Sss… kind of. Why? Did…"

He shook his head before leaning down to trace the tip of his tongue over the love bite, rather torn by the contradictory feelings sweeping through him. He felt bad for her sake, that she was hurt; but he also felt cocky about the thoroughness of his kisses. It was obvious to him that Shreya was a complete novice, though her enthusiasm more than compensated for her lack of experience.

She reached out with her tongue to check her lower lip at exactly the moment he swept his tongue soothingly over the area. Gasping with the escalating sensations, she drew his tongue into her mouth and sucked on it greedily.

With a loud groan, Chirag gathered her into his arms before returning her gesture passionately. His hands moved restlessly over her slender back as he drew her closer to his hard chest, groaning some more when he felt her soft and luscious breasts pressing against the front of his body. *What will she do if I touch her breast?* Putting thought to action, he raised a hand to cup her left breast, squeezing it gently. He was thrilled to feel the nipple hardening and nudging against his palm, making him ravenous for more. "Shrey…"

"Mmm…" Without even being aware of what she was doing, Shreya thrust her breast into his palm, making mewling noises from deep down her throat.

He stroked his thumb repeatedly over the turgid tip, letting go of her mouth to kiss the rapidly beating pulse at her throat. "Shrey… I want you." He spoke to her in a heated whisper, nibbling on her ear.

"I want you too." Pushing away from him with great difficulty—it wasn't easy to lift herself out of the steaming passionate glaze she seemed to have sunken into—she pressed her palms to his chest. "Chirag!"

"What?" He gazed down at her, his coal black eyes gleaming in the light which came from the street lamp outside the compound wall.

"I think it's best I go home."

"No!" He wasn't ready to let go of her yet as his body protested painfully. He wanted to make her his, at least for the night.

She shook her head. "Listen, Chirag. Your parents…"

He groaned, shaking his head as he placed his hand over her mouth to stop her from speaking further. "Damn! I forgot all about them." Studying her face, he shook his head once again. "I'd better get you an ice pack."

"Why?" She looked up at him, a small frown puckering her neat forehead.

"I don't think you want to know." A glimmer of a smile appeared on his tense face.

"Tell me." She spoke firmly, giving him a mock glare, unable to stop the answering smile which lit up her face. He looked so adorable, his handsome face appearing rough with his hair all tumbled over his broad forehead along with the dark fuzz on his lean cheeks. The heat and desire in his eyes called out to the wild side in her, making her want to throw all caution to the winds and simply surrender to his demands.

"Your lips are red and swollen. Does this hurt?" he asked once again, touching the right corner of her lower lip.

"It stings," she admitted.

He sighed. "Exactly why you need an ice pack. Let me go and get one."

"You mean I'm in no fit state to meet your parents to wish them 'goodbye'?" she asked, widening her eyes in a fake innocent expression.

He grimaced. "Exactly."

She laughed. "Are you aware how wild you appear?" she asked him cheekily.

"Eh?" He frowned at her mischievous face, torn between frustration and amusement. "Why?"

She reached over to press her hands on the open flaps of his shirt, the top four buttons having come undone, all thanks to her ministrations. "Let me help you button up your shirt. I don't think you want anyone to see the hickeys on your chest." She gurgled with laughter as she reached over to press her lips to two different points on his chest.

"What?" *Did she mention hickeys?* His eyes went wide with amazement. He looked down at himself, astounded to see the red marks on his own chest. "Vixen!" He crushed her in his arms, feeling more aroused than ever.

She gave a muffled giggle before asking, "Shall I help you with the buttons?"

"I suppose you'd better," he muttered.

Stepping away from him, she pulled the flaps of his shirt together before pushing the buttons into their slots.

When she reached his throat, he held her forearms firmly to stop her from continuing. "Are you planning to choke me?" he asked.

Lifting her gaze from the task at hand, she looked up into his dark eyes. "Of course not."

"Then leave the top button alone."

"Okay." She patted his chest to let him know that the job was done. "Shall we go? It's getting rather late."

"You wait right here. Let me get the ice pack." He left her under the tree close to the compound wall to walk quickly to the back door which led into the kitchen; and was back within a couple of minutes. "Here." He pressed the ice cube wrapped in a soft cloth to her lower lip. "I'm sorry, sweetheart."

Her brown eyes danced with amusement when she lifted them up to his. Shaking her head, she said, "I'm not."

He threw the ice pack down on the ground to grab her close to his chest, burying his face in the crook of her neck. "You tempt me like crazy."

"Do you want to make love to me?" she asked, her voice a soft whisper in his ear. She reached with the tip of her tongue to touch his earlobe, fascinated by the texture. Not stopping to think, she nipped his lobe, just the way he had nibbled on hers earlier. She let go immediately, startled when she heard his loud groan. "I'm sorry. Did I hurt you?" she asked, continuing to whisper.

He shook his head. "No. No, you didn't hurt me; more like unmanned me."

She shut her eyes for a moment, trying to grasp the meaning of his words. When she still couldn't comprehend what he meant, she opened her eyes to ask, "I don't understand. What did I do?"

His face tight with longing, he shook his head from side to side. "I think it's better I take you home."

She stamped her foot when sudden fury burst forth from within her. Twin brown flames pinned him down as she accused, "Not fair, Chirag. What did I do different from what you did to me? It was okay when you kissed my ear. But I can't do the same to you?"

His mouth fell open in amazement when he saw the furious virago in the place of the sweet young woman he had been kissing barely a couple of minutes ago. Her temper drove him nuts, making him desire her all the more. Her face was a sight! Her hair tumbled about her slender shoulders, the curls no less than a riot. Her eyebrows were puckered in a deep scowl which only made her appear more passionate than angry. As for her brown eyes, they appeared like twin flames which lit a fire in him. The nostrils of her slim nose were flared while her lush mouth was pouted in displeasure.

She completely lost it when he didn't respond. Clenching her hands into tight fists, she lifted them to rain blows on his chest, finding infinite pleasure in giving vent to the raging passion which he had invoked.

"Stop it! Stop it, Shreya!" It was funny to begin with, until he felt the sting of her blows which soon became painful. "You're hurting me."

"You poor baby!" she snarled, baring her small teeth at him.

Astonishment, amusement, and desire warred within him as Chirag wrapped his large hands around her small fists, holding them firmly against his chest. "Don't you have a temper?!"

"So, what did you think? That I'm a pussycat who will wrap myself around your leg?" she snarled, trying to remove her fists from his hold. Damn it! He wasn't even holding her hands tightly, but she still couldn't free herself.

He burst out laughing when his imagination brought the scene to life—of Shreya wrapping herself around his leg. "Not a pussycat, no! More like a tigress." *My tigress!*

Her anger evaporated as swiftly as it had appeared while she stared up at him, pacified by his words. And his laughter brought an answering smile to her face. With a soft sigh, she wrapped her arms around his lean waist before laying her head on his chest, revelling in the steady beat of his heart.

It was a long time before Chirag drove her home, once Shreya said her 'goodbyes' to his parents, her face a study in calmness.

7

Shreya entered her bedroom quietly, only to give a startled yelp when she saw Aadhira sitting on her bed, fiddling with her phone.

"Heya, Shrey! Where have you been?" asked Aadhira, winking at her older sister. While there was a gap of three years between the two, they were extremely close. Aadhira was still in college, but had jumped in when her parents planned this trip to Delhi, managing to convince her department professor that she would continue to study during the trip. The professor had agreed only because Aadhira was one of the more brilliant students in her class.

Shreya's eyes glittered with excitement as she grinned at her sister, placing a finger on her lips to silence Aadhira. Walking back to the door, she pushed the lock in place before returning to sit on her bed, facing Aadhira. "I went out with Chirag."

"Again?" asked Aadhira, dropping her phone beside her on the bed to sit up and give her sister all her attention. "Wait! Before you say something, did he kiss you?" she asked, staring at Shreya's swollen mouth. She didn't miss the extra redness at one corner.

Colour flared on Shreya's face as she gave a small nod, her eyes continuing to shine brightly. She lifted a hand to stop her sister from speaking, and said, "Wait! Let me answer your questions before you ask me some more. Yes, I went out with Chirag, again. In fact, I went to his house for dinner, mainly to meet his cats. I…"

Aadhira squealed in delight. "You met Jack and Jill? How cute are they? Did…"

Shreya glared at her younger sibling, or at least tried to, but her lips gave her away as they split into a wide smile. "They are even cuter than I imagined."

"But how come you went to his house? His parents had gone out or what?" asked Aadhira, dying of curiosity.

Shreya shook her head. "They both were there. But listen, it was okay. Chirag introduced me as a friend. I don't think they expect anything to happen between us."

"But obviously something did happen," declared Aadhira, her dark brown eyes glowing with excitement. "Tell me all."

"Only if you allow me," grumbled Shreya.

"Okay, I won't utter another word," promised Aadhira, placing a hand over her mouth, as she looked at her sister avidly.

"After dinner, Chirag and I went for a walk in the garden. And we kissed. That's all." Shreya got up to change out of her clothes and into her nightshirt, refusing to meet her sister's shrewd gaze.

Aadhira jumped to her feet to place her hands on Shreya's shoulders to shake her hard. "You can't stop with that. How can you say 'that's all'? What did he exactly do? How did you respond? And don't tell me you both shared one simple kiss. You look like he… he ravaged your mouth."

"What? Ravaged?" Shreya burst out laughing, her whole body shaking with mirth. "Where the hell did you hear that word? It sounds ancient."

"Discovered it in one of those historical fictions I keep reading," muttered Aadhira. "Wait, you can't change the subject like that. I want to know everything."

With a dramatic sigh, Shreya plonked down on her bed before facing her sister. "Okay, we shared more than one kiss. And then he brought me back home." She had to stop herself from laughing out loud when she saw the abject disappointment on Aadhira's face.

"Nooooo…" Aadhira protested. "Tell me how it was. Come on, Shrey! This is your favourite sis asking," she said, in her best pleading tone. "Pretty please," she added for good measure.

Shreya shook her head. "It's a little too personal."

Aadhira jumped to her feet and went to sit next to Shreya, throwing an arm around her shoulders. "Come on, Shrey. Just a little more. You are the eldest. If you don't share your experience with me, how will I know when my time comes?" She fluttered her eyelashes at her sister beseechingly.

Shreya rolled her eyes to the ceiling and back. "Exactly how I am learning, on the job."

"So, how was the job? Did your heart go pitter patter? Did you become breathless? Did… er… did your breasts feel all tingly as they say in books?" Aadhira decided to change her line of questioning, hoping to get some answers now.

Shreya turned to look at her younger sister, realising that she wasn't going to get away with not answering. "It was all that, and more." She bit her tongue when she realised her mistake.

"Aah! And what exactly does 'and more' cover?"

"I'm tired, Aadhi." Shreya pretended to yawn widely, covering her mouth with one hand. "It's past one, you know."

"I know. Which is exactly why I am asking you all these questions. Do you realise that you left home before six? Which is all of seven hours. You…"

Shreya placed her hand over her sister's mouth to stop her from speaking further. "Chirag is an amazing kisser. And I loved it, okay?"

"Didn't he ask to sleep with you?"

"No, he didn't." Shreya lay on the bed, trying to push her sister off it with her foot, without any success.

"But why?" Aadhira asked, a fierce scowl on her face.

"Are you mad, Aadhi? We barely know each other."

"You mean there is a chance that he might ask you in the near future?" A romantic at heart, Aadhira wanted her sister to have a fairy tale happily-ever-after. And she hadn't missed the sparkle in Shreya's eyes whenever she took Chirag Bhatia's name.

"Only he knows what he is going to do in the future," bit out Shreya, punching her pillow with a tight little fist before turning on her front, shutting her eyes firmly.

"You mean you're going to let him call all the shots?" asked Aadhira, surprised to hear Shreya's defeated tone.

Shreya sat up with a jerk, glaring at Aadhira. "What do you want me to do? Invite him to bed?" she snarled.

"Maybe not in so many words. But I suppose you can lead him there…" Aadhira gave her sister a naughty smile.

"Is that the voice of experience talking?" asked Shreya, returning her younger sibling's smile with a sly one of her own.

"Hahaha! I wish."

"I think you should go back to your bed and let me sleep."

"Why? You want to dream of more kisses, do you?" Aadhira was nothing if not persistent.

"Aadhi!" Shreya slapped her sister's arm playfully. "Go!"

"Okay, I'm going. Goodnight."

"Goodnight," responded Shreya in a muffled voice, as she had already tugged the comforter over her face. But sleep was a long time in coming as she couldn't stop thinking of the steamy kisses she had shared with Chirag earlier. She smiled to herself when she realised she had lost count after the first two. It was a good thing she had refused to answer that particular question of Aadhira's.

Will he call me tomorrow? Or should I text him? It was obvious from the bulge in his jeans that Chirag had wanted to make love to her fully. And he had been miffed they were at his family home. But then, he had made no suggestions for meeting the next day, nor had he invited her to his bachelor pad.

A soft sigh escaped Shreya's lips as she rolled to the other side, punching her pillow some more. She refused to rise to the bait when she heard Aadhira's giggle, though she couldn't stop a smile from stretching her lips.

Taking deep breaths to clear her mind of thoughts, she focused on Jack and Jill and the time she had spent with them. Thankfully, sleep claimed her not long after.

"Shit!" Chirag lifted his startled gaze to stare at his body in the mirror, his eyes drawn to the couple of teeth marks on the left side of his chest. It was Saturday morning and he remembered making a vague promise to take Shreya and her siblings to the swimming pool at his club. He had planned to invite them over around mid-morning, and stay back for lunch.

But how could he show himself at the swimming pool with these red marks which stood out like beacons? It wouldn't have mattered with his friends, who were bound to be there too. But this wasn't how he had envisaged meeting Shreya's sister and brothers. It would be too damn awkward.

He felt torn between disappointment and relief that he would have to cancel their swimming date. Disappointment, because he wouldn't be able to meet her. Relief, all because of his hesitation to take her to bed after realising she was probably a virgin. He didn't want to be the one to take away her innocence. Picking up his phone, he called Shreya. "Hey, good morning, Shrey!"

"Good morning," greeted Shreya, with a total lack of enthusiasm. "I was just going to call you."

"Regarding our swimming session? Which is exactly why I called. I'm sorry, Shrey, but I can't go swimming. I…"

Just what she had expected. After all, hadn't he gone silent after her dinner at the Bhatias' residence two days ago? No, she wasn't going to think of the kisses they had shared—ones which had made her brain go numb. But not any longer. Shreya was completely alert, with all her faculties intact. No way was she going to be fooled by a handsome man with pretty manners. "That's perfect. As I can't go either. Today, my parents and I are going to lunch with the Choksi family. They have a son of marriageable age. Have you heard of the Choksis who own some popular jewellery brand? Their shop is in

Connaught Place, I believe." She deliberately gave him as many details as she herself knew. Why not? Let Chirag not imagine she was pining after him.

"Choksi Jewellers?" he asked, a heavy frown on his face. "I've heard of them." *I am sure their son must be a wimp,* thought Chirag to himself, his jaw clenching at the idea of Shreya going to meet yet another prospective bridegroom. How could she do that, after kissing him senseless only two days ago? He conveniently forgot the way he had avoided her soon after that.

"I think so," said Shreya, wondering if he was going to say something about it. After the steamy kisses they had shared on Thursday, there had been no contact from Chirag. He had neither called her nor messaged her. While she had been under the impression he wanted to make love to her, she couldn't bring herself to ask him outright. Well, how did a girl ask a guy if he still wanted to have sex with her? As far as she was concerned, she was too damn attracted to Chirag, and was totally ready to give up her virginity if it meant she could go to bed with him. Only, he had not bothered to message or call her, not even once, until now. And the reason he was calling her now: to cancel their tentative plan to go to his club. Damn the man! Why did he even bother?

Ambika had told her the earlier evening about the lunch they had been invited to at the Choksis' home. While Shreya hadn't protested, she had been holding on to the hope that she would hear from Chirag, only to be deeply disappointed. Refusing to give in to the hurt she felt, she had straightened her shoulders and decided to carry on with life as if nothing had happened between her and Chirag. As if her body and mind didn't feel they had both been run through the wringer that evening after dinner with the Bhatias.

"But… but I don't understand. Why are you doing this?" Chirag wanted to shout in frustration. He had barely slept the last two nights and had so been looking forward to go swimming with Shreya, even if her siblings were going to be there for company. In fact, he had been banking on her sister and brothers to keep him from throwing himself into Shreya's arms. That's how desperate he was!

"Doing what?" she asked, scowling at the view from her balcony, her eyes unseeing as she stared at the tops of the trees lining the lane she lived in.

"Going through the rigmarole of meeting prospective bridegrooms! What else?"

She shrugged, forgetting he wouldn't be able to see her. "That's what my mother wants."

"What about you? Do you want to keep meeting men randomly? Give them false hope?" Chirag snarled, in a raring temper now. He simply couldn't stand the idea of any man looking at Shreya in that light—one of a prospective bride. Grr!

"What will you have me do? If I say no, my mother will be down my throat. I…"

"What if you aren't able to escape this time? What if things get steamrollered and your marriage gets fixed?"

Which thought had been niggling at Shreya the whole of last night. That is, during the time when she hadn't been thinking of Chirag and his steamy kisses; his hand at her breast, his manhood thrusting against her abdomen. Damn it all! "What does it matter to you?" she asked him in a grumpy tone. "I don't think you care, do you?" she added for good measure.

"Shrey! That's not fair. I..."

"What's not fair, Chirag? You didn't bother to get in touch with me after Thursday evening at your place. And you're accusing me of being unfair?" She was shouting by now.

The colour left Chirag's face when he admitted to himself that she was absolutely right. But then, he had needed time to think, explore his body's explosive reaction to her proximity; his mind's total obsession with her. He had not got any work done the whole of Friday, thinking of the beautiful, intelligent, and sexy Shreya Udhas from Durban. He had been thoroughly distracted by thoughts of her responses to his lovemaking, his body hard and tight from the time she had arrived at his home for dinner, until... until this moment. Which was why he had decided to keep some distance, to get things in perspective. The women he had had affairs with before — they all knew the score. They had been aware it was going to be a temporary fling. But Shreya was another matter altogether, so obviously innocent. He was sure she had never even kissed any man before, which made it obvious she was a virgin.

"Listen, Shrey, I..."

"I need to go and get ready. Or I'll be late."

He was desperate, torn between his desire for her, and his sense of morality; that he didn't have the right to take her virginity. Then again, he didn't want her to meet any man with the idea of marriage. He simply couldn't stand the thought of any other man touching her, not even with his gaze, let alone his hands. Chirag groaned loudly before asking her, his tone almost begging, "Can't I change your mind? I..."

"What do you suggest I do?" she asked, sarcasm tingeing her voice. She was sure he had no solution to offer, not after the way he had ignored her until this morning; after kissing her senseless. Bastard! He had told her that he wanted to make love to her, and she had waited all of yesterday for him to invite her to his bachelor pad. After ignoring her for thirty-six hours, he had the audacity to tell her how to lead her life. No way! When there was no immediate response from him, she repeated what she had said earlier, "I need to go. Bye!"

"Shrey…"

Shreya cut the call, a determined thrust to her small chin. There was no way she was going to agree to marry the Choksi boy. But Chirag need not know that. Let him stew for a bit! It would do him good, as it was obvious he seemed to take her for granted. He apparently expected her to jump whenever he snapped his fingers. She wasn't a toy for him to pack into a box until the time he brought it out to play with whenever the fancy took him. Pressing the button to make her phone go silent when she saw him calling her again, Shreya left the phone on a side table in the main hall before going to her room to change.

Aadhira, who had been watching the way Shreya was snapping into the phone, walked over to see who was trying to call her again. Seeing Chirag's name on the screen, she took the call.

"Listen, Shrey! I don't quite know what has got you in a tizzy, but I…"

"Hey, I'm Aadhira, Shreya's sister."

"Oh!"

"Hello, Chirag, good to talk to you after hearing so much about you," said Aadhira, her manner friendly.

Not sure of how he should respond, Chirag said, "Hello to you too."

"Okay, listen. I need to be quick about this, before Shreya catches me and snaps my head off. Tell me something. Why didn't you bother to even call her yesterday? My sis was super disappointed when she didn't hear from you."

Ouch! Of course, she was disappointed. Why the hell hadn't he thought about that? "Is she badly pissed off with me?" he asked, sitting down on the edge of his bed, finally relaxing after the conversation he had had with Shreya. It looked like he had an ally in her younger sister.

"She is, yes," answered Aadhira truthfully.

"Damn! I hope she doesn't agree to marry the Choksi boy simply out of spite," he muttered, forgetting for a moment that there was someone at the other end listening avidly to his words.

"What?" Aadhira laughed softly. "I don't think you need to worry on that score. Shreya has no plans of getting married, not to a stranger anyway. And come on, she's barely twenty-two. Who gets married at such a young age?"

"Then why the hell is she going to meet this fellow?" growled Chirag, jumping to his feet again when his temper soared.

"You don't know our mother, do you? Or you wouldn't have asked this question," said Aadhira, an irritated note in her voice.

"I don't understand."

"Our mother is determined to make use of this trip to Delhi to fix Shreya's marriage into a family living here in India. Right now, that's the sole purpose of her life. And Shreya being Shreya, she doesn't want to hurt Mom and is simply going with the flow. The trouble is that Delhi seems to be so damn full of eligible bachelors," bit out Aadhira.

"What?" Chirag didn't know if he should be angry or amused at her comment on Delhi bachelors.

"You heard me. We have so many relatives and friends who are keen to introduce Shreya to families with prospective bridegrooms. She escaped in the first instance only because Nishant Ahuja was already in love with someone else. Now, we need to see how it goes with Kunal Choksi…"

"I'm going to choke the daylights out of this Choksi fellow," growled Chirag, prowling around his bedroom furiously.

"Why would you do that?"

"Because…" He paused, realising he had been going to say it was because he wanted Shreya for himself. But that was the wrong answer. It was bound to make Aadhira believe he wanted to marry Shreya himself. No way! Chirag was not interested in tying the knot, with Shreya or with any other woman. All he wanted was an affair, only with Shreya, it seemed. He felt no attraction to any other woman. Which brought him right back to square one when he concluded it wasn't fair on his part to take advantage of an innocent woman, all for his selfish needs.

"Because?" Aadhira prompted, turning her back to the balcony to keep an eye on any movement from the bedroom she shared with Shreya, just in case her sister popped out suddenly to see Aadhira speaking on Shreya's phone. "Are you jealous?" she asked him outright.

Damn it! She was right. Yes, he was jealous. Chirag was jealous of every man who might come within speaking distance of Shreya. "Can you stop Shreya from going to this lunch with the Choksis?" he asked, his voice pleading.

"Why would I do that?" asked Aadhira, all innocence, while her eyes danced merrily. It was obvious that this Chirag Bhatia had the hots for her sister and wasn't sure about how to deal with it.

"Because I asked you to?" he said in a hopeful voice, though he didn't really set much store in Aadhira agreeing to his request.

Aadhira laughed. "I wish I could help you, Chirag. But Mom will kill Shreya if she doesn't go today." Which was an exaggeration, but Chirag need not know that. While Ambika was determined to get her daughter married off, she would never dream of forcing Shreya into doing something she didn't want to do.

Damn! And a double damn! Chirag was flummoxed as to how to deal with the situation.

"But just as I mentioned earlier…" Aadhira paused when she noticed her mother step into the hall.

"What?"

"You can rest assured that Shreya is never going to agree to marry this Kunal Choksi," concluded Aadhira in a fierce whisper, her gaze fixed on her mother.

"Are you sure?" he asked. Aadhira was only repeating what she had mentioned earlier, and Chirag so wanted to believe her words, as he swung between hope and despair.

"I know my sister. She has no plans of getting married in the near future for one thing…"

"And for another?" He stopped pacing to listen carefully.

"She's too damn attracted to you, Chirag. Can't you see that?"

"Yes!" He pumped his fist in the air, feeling so light all of a sudden. "Thanks, Aadhira. I owe you one."

"I'm Aadhi to my friends."

"Aadhi it is. I can't wait to meet you."

"Ditto! Listen, I'd better go, before Shreya catches me on her phone."

"Bye. Oh, by the way! Do ping me from your phone. I can do with a friend residing close to Shreya."

Aadhira laughed gaily. "Sure, will do that. Bye!"

8

"**N**amaste, Sunil*ji*, Ambika*ji*, welcome to our home," greeted Anand Choksi, a broad smile on his face as he shook Sunil Udhas's hand firmly. "This is my wife, Deepa," he introduced.

"*Namaste!*" said Sunil, smiling at the couple, as he studied both their faces. It took him but a few seconds to realise that neither Anand, nor Deepa Choksi, appeared to be happy. While they showed their teeth in a wide smile, it didn't really show in their eyes. It was an effort, but somehow Sunil Udhas kept a frown from forming on his face. "This is my wife, Ambika, and that is Shreya, my eldest child," he introduced in turn.

The Udhas family followed the Choksi couple into the living room which was crammed with expensive furniture draped in silk upholstery, and a lot of artefacts covering every nook and cranny.

Ambika took her daughter's hand in hers, hiding the grimace which formed on her face as she studied the room openly.

"Sit down, please," invited Deepa, pointing to a three-seater sofa. Turning towards the back of the apartment, she called out in a loud voice, "Ganga, cold drinks *leke aao*." Turning back to the guests, she said,

"Kunal should be with us in a few minutes. He had to attend an unexpected phone call."

"No problem," said Ambika, sitting straight on the sofa, even as she wondered where Rekha and her husband were. Rekha was the one who had introduced her to the Ahujas. She was also the one who was trying to set up a match with the Choksis now. "Did Rekha mention when she is coming?" she asked Deepa.

"She should be arriving any moment, I'm sure," said Deepa, before turning to study Shreya. "What is your name, *beta*?" she asked in a saccharine sweet voice, giving the younger woman a fake smile.

"I'm Shreya," responded Shreya briefly, answering to the point. Her mind was in a whirl as she wondered how she was going to escape this alliance. The first time, during the meeting set up with Nishaan Ahuja, she hadn't thought ahead, for two reasons. One was because she had focused on the fact that things were very much in her control and she would somehow escape the alliance. And most unexpectedly, things had worked out too easily. Now, she was a mite worried the second time might not be so lucky. After all, how often would Lady Luck favour her?

Also, now that she had met Chirag, and found herself deeply attracted to him, she simply hated the idea of meeting another man in the name of an alliance. She gritted her teeth so hard that her jaw ached.

The maid brought some cold drinks. While Sunil and Ambika accepted the orange juice, obviously from a bottle, Shreya refused. "I would like to have some water, please."

Deepa laughed, patting Shreya on her shoulder. "You are so much like me. I also prefer water to these fizzy drinks," she said, before laughing once again.

Shreya looked at Deepa Choksi, wondering if something was wrong with the woman. What had she found funny that she had to laugh so much?

"Are you very shy?" asked Deepa, out of the blue.

Ambika held her daughter's hand tightly, worried Shreya might declare outright that she didn't have a timid bone in her body.

Aware of her mother's warning clutch on her hand, Shreya gave Deepa a sheepish smile and a small nod.

Deepa laughed once again, saying, "*Na, beta*. There's no need for you to feel shy. *Apna hi ghar samajna*. Are you still in college?" she asked.

Why the hell was the woman laughing so often? Shreya couldn't help feeling irritated and judgemental. "I finished college two years ago, ma'am."

"Oh, really! That's so cool!" exclaimed Deepa, "And what do you do nowadays? I'm sure your mother must have prepared you for being the perfect daughter-in-law, no? You must have learned to cook, and keep house. Wonderful! Wonderful!" Turning to Ambika, Deepa said, "I can see that you NRIs are way smarter than those families who live right here in India. You know how to train your daughters to become perfect housewives. I truly appreciate it." Hearing the woman, someone could be mistaken for thinking that Deepa didn't belong to 'those families' living in India.

Shreya turned to look at her mother, a small scowl drawing her eyebrows together, her brown eyes flaring in irritation.

Ambika turned to give her daughter a pathetic glance. She had never expected such an attitude from Deepa Choksi. Nothing her friend Rekha had mentioned had prepared her for this. The Choksi family owned a jewellery shop, in the posh locality of Connaught Place, of all areas. How come they wanted a daughter-in-law who was trained in keeping house? It was Ambika's turn to grit her teeth as she lifted her gaze to her husband who was chatting away merrily with Anand Choksi, the two of them having kept the cold drinks aside to enjoy the bottle of Scotch which resided on a table next to their host.

Feeling his wife's heated gaze on him, Sunil turned around to lift an eyebrow in enquiry, as he wondered about the annoyance on her face.

Ambika gave a small shake of her head, unable to voice her thoughts, as she continued to wonder what was keeping Rekha.

The doorbell rang as if on cue and in walked Rekha and her husband Harjeet. "Hello," they called out in greeting before the six older people began to all speak together.

Shreya, who was sitting in the middle of the sofa between her parents, fisted her hands in frustration. The first time she had done this, it had all been in fun. But not this time. This visit to the Choksis home was a stupid mistake. Chirag had been right in trying to stop her. She had not even met Kunal Choksi, but she was already nervous about the end result of today's luncheon here. She called herself all kinds of an idiot when Rekha stepped up to her to pull her into a standing position.

"Shreya, my dear!" Rekha hugged the younger woman, even as she wondered what was wrong with the Udhas family. The other day, Shreya had been dressed in a heavily embroidered *salwar kameez* in rani pink along with half a kilo of jewellery. Today, she was wearing a brilliant orange *ghagra choli* which was also heavily embroidered. The diamonds she wore on her neck and ears were enough to blind everyone within a half kilometre radius. As it was, this Deepa Choksi seemed a little crazy, as she kept laughing like a mad woman, at anything and everything. It was truly a difficult task, bringing a boy and girl together in marriage. While Rekha and her husband Harjeet had made it their life's mission to bring as many couples together in holy matrimony as was possible. Phew! What all sacrifices they had to make for the sake of society! That it was also a business which helped them earn in lakhs was something they didn't proclaim too loudly.

"Hello, Rekha Aunty," greeted Shreya, giving the other woman a glance from under her eyelashes. It was the best way to convince anyone that she was a shy, tongue-tied young lady. One surefire way of avoiding making conversation.

"You look so beautiful," declared Rekha, a fake smile on her face. "I know that Kunal is going to simply fall in love with you."

Deepa giggled as if Rekha had cracked a funny joke. "You think so? Now where is that boy? He promised to finish his call soon. *Che!* The youngsters of today! They truly don't have a sense of time. Let me go and bring him."

Right then, a slim, young man stepped out of a room on the opposite side to the entrance. He stopped in his tracks as if to check who all had arrived at his home, obviously not having expected so many people for lunch. Sweeping his dark gaze around the hall, he paused when he met his mother's eyes, and walked towards her.

"Kunal, *mera bachcha!* Come, let me introduce everyone to you. You know Rekha, of course."

"Yes. Hello, Rekha Aunty, I hope you are well. And Harjeet Uncle," Kunal shook the other man's hand with a welcoming smile on his face.

"This here is Ambika—Aunty to you—and Sunil*ji*—you must call him Uncle. And this is the lovely Shreya, their daughter. Shreya, look here," she snapped her fingers in front of Shreya's face, not bothered she had startled the younger woman so badly that Shreya looked up with a sudden jerk, nearly spraining her neck. "This is my son, Kunal Choksi. Isn't he handsome?"

Warm colour washed across Kunal's cheeks as he stared at Shreya for barely a second before dropping his gaze to the floor. There were many times when his mother had embarrassed him with her wild statements. But this classic introduction truly took the cake!

Shreya brought her eyelids down to hide the amusement in her eyes. Poor Kunal Choksi. It was a wonder he did not die of embarrassment whenever his mother was around. She felt so damn sorry for the man.

Ambika turned to meet her daughter's laughing eyes for a moment, her own glittering with mirth, before turning towards Deepa Choksi. "You are absolutely right, Deepa. Kunal is indeed a handsome man," she agreed in a polite voice.

Rekha grinned amiably at both her friends—Ambika and Deepa. "Mark my words, ladies. These two, Kunal and Shreya, will make a perfectly beautiful match."

Deepa laughed as if it was the funniest joke, clapping her hands together, making Shreya convinced that the woman was mad, at least a little, if not fully.

Noticing that things were slowly sliding out of control, Kunal's father, Anand, spoke in a loud voice. "Why don't we all move to the dining room? Let's not allow the food to grow cold."

"I agree." Rekha's husband Harjeet responded in a relieved voice, as they all turned around to walk towards the doorway which obviously led to the dining area.

Everyone settled down, once Rekha made sure Shreya was seated next to Kunal, giving them both a sly wink and a broad smile.

Shreya grimaced as she lifted the colourful cloth napkin before spreading it over her lap, refusing to glance to her right where Kunal was seated.

"Hello," said Kunal, his voice barely a whisper as he tilted his head towards her.

"Hey," she responded, turning to look at him. He was good looking. But wasn't he a bit too young to be thinking of marriage? Her tongue running away with her, she asked, "How old are you?"

It was Kunal's turn to grimace. "Twenty-four. You?"

"Twenty-two. Do you really want to marry so young?" asked Shreya outright.

He gave a small shake of his head, passing the bowl of *kadhi* towards her. "Of course not."

She breathed a small sigh of relief. "Then why did you agree to this meeting?" she asked, though she was sure she already knew the answer.

"You met my mother," he said, a scowl on his forehead, "Do you think I had a choice here?"

Shreya burst out laughing, unable to stop herself. Was this the problem with all the youngsters in Indian households? Being crushed under the thumbs of their parents? Even in her case, while her mother wouldn't exactly force her, Ambika was definitely bulldozing Shreya to follow her plans. Okay, maybe to only an extent, but it was still parental pressure.

Rekha took Ambika's hand in hers and squeezed hard. "This is going to work, don't you think? I know it, deep down in my heart," she declared.

Ambika also nodded her agreement, a smile on her face when she looked at her daughter chatting with Kunal Choksi. A small frown gathered on her forehead after a few moments. The boy appeared so damn young. Would he be able to keep pace with Shreya? After all, her daughter was kind of grown up for her age. Ambika wondered if it would make better sense if Shreya had a mature partner who would be able to keep up with her. Turning her gaze back to Rekha, she asked, "How old is he?"

"Twenty-four, almost twenty-five," said Rekha. "Your daughter is twenty-two, right? This will be a perfect match; you mark my words."

Ambika was already shaking her head in denial, confident by now, this was never going to work. Shreya would run circles around the man within a week of marriage. And where would that leave them all?

"Do you wanna go to a party this evening?" asked Kunal.

Why did he want her to go with him? Hadn't he just now mentioned he wasn't keen to get married? Shreya lifted an eyebrow at him, as she bit into a piece of *roti* wrapped around *mattar paneer*. She didn't really have to ask him the question 'why'.

He shrugged in response. "I am being selfish here. It would help me if I appeared to make an effort to get to know you."

It was a good thing the dining table was big enough to seat twelve people, and there was no one sitting on either side of the two youngsters. Which was exactly what Rekha had planned. No one could hear what Kunal and Shreya were whispering to one another.

Shreya gave him a nod and a small smile, even as she wondered how she was going to convince her parents this alliance was entirely unsuitable. Maybe, what Kunal suggested might work towards her cause too. Thinking quickly on her feet, she said, "Okay."

"Great! Let me pick you up at your place. Eight o' clock works for you?"

"Is it going to be a late-night party?" Shreya's eyes went wide in enquiry.

He shrugged once again. "Yeah. Many of my friends are working this Saturday. So! What do you say?"

"Okay, I suppose. Where are we going?"

"To a friend's bungalow in Gurugram. Are you familiar with the area?" he asked, his dark gaze on hers as he spooned some *kadhi* into his mouth.

"I've heard of it."

"Eight o' clock then?"

"How are we getting there?" she asked, a wary expression on her face. At the end of the day, Kunal was a complete stranger. No, she refused to dwell on the fact that Chirag had also been a stranger, until they got to know each other.

"We'll take a cab. I don't drink and drive," he said, giving her a cocky smile, confident he must have impressed her with his lofty principle.

Shreya gave a small nod. "Okay."

"So, it's a date?" he asked, his smile wider now.

She lifted an eyebrow once again, wondering what he was trying to prove. "It's not exactly a date, is it? More like pulling the wool over your mother's eyes."

"I hope you aren't too disappointed."

"About what?" she asked, a frown drawing her eyebrows together in the middle of her forehead.

"That we aren't going to get married. I'm sorry about it, but…"

"It's okay, Kunal," said Shreya briefly. She wasn't going to let on about her feeling of relief that he didn't want to be married, at least not anytime soon.

"But you must have come here with a lot of hopes, dreams…" he paused, not missing the amusement in her gaze before she lowered it to her plate.

"You shouldn't worry. We are strangers, after all." But she was still ready to go out with him that evening, just so her mother wouldn't bother her some more about the match which was not going to work out.

It was another hour before they took leave of the Choksis. Shreya sat inside the car first, hoping her mother was not going to bombard her with questions.

"I think that boy is too young for our Shreya," said Ambika, much to her daughter's surprise.

"You think so?" asked Sunil, turning to the back where Ambika and Shreya were seated.

"Yes, he is barely twenty-four." Turning to her daughter, she said, "You both seemed to get along well, though."

Shreya shrugged. "We couldn't exactly pick up a quarrel, could we?" she muttered, not caring that she was being sarcastic. Raising her voice, she said, "I'm going to a party with Kunal tonight."

Ambika grimaced. "Do you really want to?"

Sunil didn't miss the amusement on his daughter's face. He was well aware that Shreya wasn't keen on being married, believing she was too young for matrimony; she was only playing along with Ambika's suggestions. "Are you sure, Shreya?" he asked.

"It might be fun."

"Don't forget to weigh all the pros and cons before making a decision, okay?" Ambika gave her daughter a worried glance. What if Shreya decided to marry Kunal Choksi?

"Mom, listen. Wouldn't it have made better sense for you to find out the man's age before setting up this lunch meeting?" It was an effort to keep the bite out of her voice when Shreya asked the question.

Ambika smote her forehead. "What to do? It is all that Rekha's doing. She told me how well educated the boy is. And what a wonderful job he was doing, assisting his father in the jewellery showroom. She also insisted you and he will make a perfect match."

"We've been in Delhi for three weeks, and already you have set up two meetings. Can we stop this farce now, please?" Shreya turned to her father after uttering the words to her mother, her gaze pleading.

"I think…"

Ambika cut her husband short when she spoke angrily. "What do you mean by calling it a farce? Here I am, using this opportunity while we are in Delhi, to find a suitable bridegroom for you. And you are making a mockery of me?"

"Mom! I feel so foolish parading from one house to another, wearing such stupid costumes. Why can't I simply enjoy my holiday in Delhi?"

Ambika turned to her husband. "Look at your daughter, Sunil. She's all of twenty-two. Isn't it time for her to get married?" she appealed.

"You were twenty-six when we got married," said Sunil, giving his daughter a wink.

Ambika growled in frustration, unable to deny his words, as he was only speaking the truth.

"Mom! You never told me that." Shreya turned to her mother, laughter in her gaze. "No more bridegroom hunting, okay? Let's have some fun, instead."

"How can you, Sunil?" Ambika glared at her husband.

Shreya ignored her parents to check the messages on her phone.

9

Chirag was at work when Nishaan called him on his phone. "Hey, bro."

"Hmm."

Nishaan removed the phone from his ear to look at the screen, as if to check if he had dialled the correct number. "Chirag? What's wrong?"

"Tch! Nothing. You tell me. Why did you call?"

Nishaan frowned. The two of them were too close and till date had never needed a specific reason to call each other. Something was definitely amiss. "Where are you? I went to your house in search of you, but…"

"At my office, where else?" Chirag growled, cutting his friend off mid-sentence.

"But today is a fourth Saturday. How come you're working?"

Chirag sighed, extra loudly. "Does a man require to explain himself, all because he wants to do some honest work?"

"Who the hell are you? And what have you done with my best friend?" asked Nishaan, only half joking. "I'm coming over to check for myself." He disconnected the phone to drive his car out of the compound of Chirag's home, wading through the Saturday afternoon traffic to reach Chirag's office. Parking the car at the visitors' parking area, he took the lift to Chibha Advertising Agency, not really surprised to find the office deserted, except for the security guard who was sitting outside the doorway.

"Good afternoon, Mr Ahuja." The man waved Nishaan in, greeting him with a smile.

"Good afternoon, Shukla. All well?" Nishaan chatted with the security guard for a couple of minutes before he walked over to Chirag's cabin and knocked on the door before pushing it open. "Which house did you belong to when you were in the fourth standard? What was the name of your first pet?"

"Very funny!" Chirag glared at Nishaan's laughing face. "Why are you here?"

"*Arre*, I've come in search of my childhood friend. But I see only his clone here. Unless you can answer those questions?" Nishaan winked.

"*Bas yaar*, Nishaan. I'm in no mood for your funny jokes," growled Chirag.

"But you agree they are funny?" Nishaan walked over to the office desk before plonking down on a visitors' chair. "Okay now. Out with it! What's up?"

"Shreya has gone bridegroom hunting, again."

"Again?"

"Isn't that what I told you just now?" Chirag frowned ferociously at Nishaan.

"Okay, okay." Nishaan spread out his palms in front of him, in a pacifying gesture, before continuing, "But then, what's so surprising about that? Isn't that their plan? To find her a suitable bridegroom while they are here in Delhi?" asked Nishaan in his most reasonable voice. He hadn't missed the fact that his best friend had been enamoured by Shreya, during the house party at the Ahujas. But according to Chirag, he was too young to take his romantic relationships seriously.

"No, damn it!" Chirag slammed his fist on his desk, the noise reverberating around the empty office.

"Eh? Are you sure? Rekha Aunty is setting up meetings for Shreya. And you know how determined she can be."

"I'm going to kill her." Chirag gritted his teeth until his jaw ached.

"Kill who? Shreya? Or Rekha Aunty?" Nishaan was having a difficult time holding back his laughter.

"Bastard! And you call yourself my friend," growled Chirag, leaning back in his chair before lifting his legs to place them on the desk. "Rekha Aunty, of course. Why will I kill Shreya? I..."

"Oh yeah! Why would you? When you lust after her so obviously?" Nishaan gave a sage nod, his eyes twinkling with mirth.

"One of these days, *na*, Nishaan, you are going to die at my hands," said Chirag, interlocking his fingers to place them over his flat abdomen as he looked at Nishaan through half closed eyes.

"Aren't you all blood thirsty suddenly? Tell you what? Let's go drinking at the club. It might help quench your thirst, if not for blood, at least for..." He let the sentence go unfinished, his meaning obvious.

"Let's go," said Chirag, getting up immediately. "I'm in the mood to get drunk."

"Perfect, come along." Nishaan pushed back his chair to get up too. He slapped Chirag on his shoulder as they stepped out of the cabin. "What's happening with you and Shreya, anyway?"

"Nothing."

"Then why are you bothered about her husband hunting?"

Chirag stopped in his tracks to glower at his best friend. "Is your plan to get a kick out of irritating me the whole evening?" he asked.

"Eh? Are you crazy? Don't forget I knew you from the time you were in your diapers. Why would I do something like that?"

Chirag shook his head, walking out of the office, totally unaware of the security guard who wished him 'goodnight'. It was left to Nishaan to answer the man before they continued towards the elevator. "Tell me something! What do you exactly feel for Chaahat?" Chirag lifted an enquiring eyebrow at his friend.

"I love her from the bottom of my heart," said Nishaan, the smile on his face turning tender. Chaahat was the woman he was going to marry. They had clashed a lot before realising they were in love with each other. They were in a relationship and planned to marry four years hence.

"I've heard that story a million times," declared Chirag in a bored voice. "What I am asking you is, what do you exactly feel? What do you mean when you say you are in love?"

Nishaan didn't answer immediately as he searched for the right words to explain his feelings for his future wife, the woman he loved from the bottom of his heart. "Chaahat is my other half, she completes me. Without her, I'll be..." he paused, once again searching for words, "I'll be a body without its soul."

Chirag's eyes went wide as he stared at his friend in amazement. It was not just Nishaan's words which hit him hard, but also the expression of abject adoration on his face. "I must say that Chaahat is truly a lucky woman," he said, in a hushed voice.

Nishaan smiled at him, shaking his head slowly from side to side. "It is I who am lucky to have her."

Deep! That's what they were—Nishaan's feelings for Chaahat. *Do I feel something similar for Shreya?* Chirag mentally shook his head. He wasn't sure. Or maybe it was too soon to tell. After all, they had met only thrice so far. While they chatted a lot, they had never had a heart-to-heart till date. Okay, they had kissed. And the kisses were damn steamy. But that only meant they were both physically compatible. Which was neither here nor there. He grimaced as his thoughts swirled around the woman who had recently entered his life. He wanted to make love to her. It was her innocence which stopped him from doing exactly that. Damn!

They left their cars back at the office park area as the friends planned to get drunk, taking a cab to the club. Nishaan looked at Chirag, unable to grasp much from his profile. His friend was staring out of the front window of the cab, unseeingly. A smile lit up Nishaan's face. It was obvious Chirag was deep in thought. About Shreya? It appeared so.

"Why the hell are you staring at me?" growled Chirag, turning around suddenly to glare at Nishaan.

"Eh?"

"Go on, tell me."

"Seriously?" Nishaan had a difficult time curbing his amusement.

"Of course, yes."

"I think you've got it bad."

"What?" Chirag turned sideways to glower at Nishaan. "What the fuck are you saying?"

"You heard me."

"But I don't understand you."

"Okay, let me be upfront. You've got the hots for Shreya. Tell me if I'm wrong."

"It's none of your goddamn business." Chirag turned away to look out of his window.

"Then I'm right."

"Will you get off my case, Nishaan?" Chirag snarled tempestuously.

Nishaan shrugged, keeping his silence. After all, there was nothing more to ask, as it was only too obvious that Chirag was deeply attracted to Shreya, if not more.

"What? Don't you have anything to say?" Chirag glared at Nishaan's profile.

Nishaan gave a dramatic sigh. "Maybe when you're in a more reasonable frame of mind."

"Do you want me to punch you? *Sala!*"

"You know you can't win over me in the boxing ring. And I don't think your Shreya will appreciate your black eye tomorrow."

Chirag punched his fist into the back of the empty passenger seat in the front, startling the cab driver. "For the first and last time, she's not my Shreya. And it's Chaahat who will be upset with your black eyes, two of them, mind you."

Unable to stop himself, Nishaan burst out laughing, slapping Chirag on his shoulder.

Chirag tried to hold on to his bad temper, but couldn't stop the smile which broke out on his face. "I'm going to give you that black eye, one of these days."

"Why? Because I dare to speak the truth?" asked Nishaan, laughing some more.

"With friends such as you, who needs an enemy?!" Chirag sat back, his posture relaxing after a long time.

They reached the Delhi Gymkhana Club and went to The Main Bar which had a truly old-world atmosphere, with comfortable sofas and cushioned chairs grouped around low tables with a lot of space in between. They chose a table at the furthest corner and settled down. Being a Saturday night, it was bound to become crowded later. Luckily, they had got here as soon as the bar opened at seven. They placed an order for whisky and soda, along with a plate of *paneer pakoras* and chicken kebabs.

"Are you going to tell me what your problem is?" asked Nishaan, a serious expression on his face as he took a sip from his glass of whisky.

"Regarding Shreya?" asked Chirag, stalling for time as he gathered his thoughts from the jumble they were in.

"Yep."

Chirag leaned his head against the sofa's backrest and stared up at the high ceiling. "Shreya's cute, she's funny. She's also extremely intelligent and I find her damn hot."

"Hmm." Nishaan popped a piece of *pakora* into his mouth as he waited for Chirag to continue, even as he wondered what the problem was.

"We kissed, you know." Chirag placed his whisky on the table, forgetting all about it as he continued to study the ceiling as if his life's lessons were all written over there.

"Oh... kay."

"It was nothing like what I'd experienced before. I…" Chirag sat up suddenly to glare at Nishaan. "Don't you dare laugh!" he threatened his friend.

"Can you see me laughing?" asked Nishaan, a serious expression on his face. He realised he was right. His friend had got it really bad.

"Okay. The problem is this. She's so damn young. And all I want is an affair. But you know I don't mess with innocents." A shuddering sigh ripped through Chirag.

Nishaan understood him only too well. He patted Chirag's shoulder, lifting the plate of kebabs and offering it to him.

Chirag munched on a piece as he stared at Nishaan. "Do you have any advice?" he asked, a wary expression on his face.

It was Nishaan's turn to stare unseeingly at the opposite wall this time as he thought over Chirag's problem. "If I'm not mistaken, Shreya is in her early twenties…"

"She's twenty-two."

"Are you sure she's innocent? In this day and age? She's from Durban too."

"I don't think she's even kissed another man properly before…" Chirag shrugged, not keen to complete the sentence.

Nishaan grimaced. His friend definitely had a point there. "What was her reaction after you kissed her?"

"Why the hell do you want to know, you bugger?" Chirag was quick to lose his temper once again.

"Idiot! I'm asking you a straightforward question here. Do you want me to help you? Or not?"

Chirag calmed down. "She was an enthusiastic participant."

"Aah! That's good. No, that's great," declared Nishaan, lifting a hand to the waiter for a refill.

"How so?" Chirag couldn't stop the feeling of hope flowering in the region of his heart.

"There's a first time for everyone, right? Why can't you be Shreya's first lover?"

"But she's out here to catch a bridegroom," grimaced Chirag, his lips drooping at the corners.

"You are mistaken, my friend. It's not she who's on the lookout for a husband, but her mother. You don't know how relieved Shreya was when I told her I already had a girlfriend."

"Oh yeah! I remember." Chirag sat up straight. "You could be right."

"I know I'm right. Which is exactly why I asked you how she reacted to your kiss. Or should I say kisses?"

"None of your business," said Chirag, but with a smile on his face as he recalled the time he had spent with Shreya in his garden. She had not only responded to his kisses enthusiastically, but also initiated a few of her own. And more than anything, she had given him, not one, but two hickeys on his chest. The reason why he had cancelled their swimming date, right here at this club.

Noticing the secretive smile on Chirag's face, Nishaan couldn't stop himself from teasing the other man. "There was way more than a simple kiss between the two of you." It was a statement, not a question.

Chirag lifted his amused gaze to meet Nishaan's laughing one. "Maybe."

"Do you think Shreya wouldn't let you make love to her? Fully, I mean."

Chirag gave a small shake of his head. "That's not the issue here. I don't want to…"

"Are you scared of making love to a virgin?" asked Nishaan, outright.

"Don't talk shit, man."

"Then?"

"I don't want to hurt her…"

"Excuse me! You will hurt her if it's her first time."

"You think you're being funny?" Chirag, who generally was of an even disposition, found his temper flying off the handle at the smallest of provocation.

"I'm only being realistic here."

"I am not talking about hurting her physically, no."

"Are you worried she might fall for you?"

Which was exactly what Chirag feared. And there was no way he could warn her off. He gave a small nod in answer to Nishaan's question.

"What about you? Is there a chance you might fall for her?"

Which was another thing which had been bothering him over the past two days. Chirag was not ready for commitment. Not for the next few years anyway. But he hadn't been able to get Shreya out of his mind from the first time he set eyes on her. Which had never happened to him before now. It wasn't as if all the girls he had wanted to take to bed, had fallen into his arms. He had won some, he had lost some. But it had never bothered him before today. Now, he was afraid of what he might be letting himself for, becoming closer to Shreya. So, it was not just Shreya he was worried about, but also himself.

Nishaan drew his own conclusions when Chirag continued to remain silent. "Shall we order dinner?"

"Hmm."

Chirag's phone rang when they were in the middle of dinner. Seeing Shreya's face on the screen, he quickly took the call, a smile of joy on his face. If she had agreed to wed that Kunal Choksi, she wouldn't be calling him, would she? "Hey, sweetheart!"

Shreya's voice was slurred when she responded briefly. "Check my message, 'kay? Bye."

His smile disappearing to be replaced with a frown, Chirag opened his WhatsApp and scrolled through the multiple messages before zeroing in on hers. "HELP! URGENT." It was followed by a location. Pushing back his chair to get up, even as he checked the location, Chirag spoke urgently to Nishaan. "I need to leave immediately. Shreya needs my help."

Nishaan wiped his hands and mouth with the cloth napkin before getting up too. "I'll go with you." He settled the bill quickly by simply signing on the paper before rushing out of the club behind Chirag who had already ordered a cab. "What happened?"

"I don't really know. But it looks like Shreya might be in some kind of trouble. The location says Gurugram."

"Might be in trouble? Don't you know for sure?" Nishaan was frowning by now, as he wondered if he had offered to go on a wild goose chase, all for nothing.

"Check this." Chirag showed Shreya's message to Nishaan.

Noticing the CAPS, Nishaan realised Chirag was probably right in believing something was amiss.

Neither man spoke much as they sat in the cab, settling in for the long ride which was bound to take them the better part of an hour.

A few minutes into the journey, a restless Chirag dialled Aadhira's phone. After all, hadn't his new friend promised to help him with anything concerning Shreya? "Hi, Aadhi."

"Hi, Chirag." Aadhira greeted him, surprise in her voice. After all, it was past ten and she had definitely not expected him to call her so late in the evening. "What's up?"

"Er… is Shrey around? I'm unable to get through to her." Chirag was not at all keen on worrying Shreya's younger sister as he uttered the white lie.

"Oh! Shreya's not at home. She's gone out with…" She paused, wondering if she should tell him about Kunal Choksi. Why bother? When she knew only too well that the information was bound to irritate Chirag.

"With?" Chirag persisted, gritting his teeth as he prayed for patience.

"Umm… Kunal Choksi. They have gone to a party somewhere in Gurugram. She…"

"Does that mean they are taking this marriage thingy forward?" asked Chirag, a dangerous note in his voice.

Aadhira shivered, even as both excitement and fear danced parallel to each other down her spine. Chirag was so obviously jealous, she thought. "No, no, it's nothing like that," she insisted in a reassuring voice. "Mom isn't at all keen on Kunal…"

"And why would that be? Wasn't it your mother's idea to meet Kunal and family?" Chirag snarled, his blood pressure increasing by the second.

"Okay, wait. Listen fully. You're right. It was Mom who arranged the meeting. But then, she realised that Kunal is too young and unsuitable for Shreya, and…"

"Then why the hell has Shreya gone out with the man?" Chirag was shouting by now, a sudden fear pervading both his body and mind. Shreya needed rescuing, urgently. While he had decided to help her out, he hadn't thought she could be in danger. But now, he wasn't so sure. It was obvious that Kunal Choksi had been rejected, at Ambika Udhas's behest. What in case the man wanted revenge? How much danger was Shreya in? If someone had mentioned that Chirag had a leaning towards drama, he would have never believed them, not before today. But right now, he wished for a pair of wings which would take him to his Shreya in a matter of seconds.

Aadhira took the phone off her ear to frown at it. Why was Chirag being so rude? That too, to her, Aadhira? She placed her phone over her ear once again to ask, "Chirag? What's wrong?"

Realising his fault immediately, Chirag took a deep breath to calm down. "I'm sorry, Aadhi. Didn't mean to shout at you."

"That's okay," said Aadhira, forgiving him immediately. "Shreya told Mom off for the bridegroom hunts she has been setting up. And insisted on going to this party, just for the heck of it. I think she just wanted to have fun, that's all."

Couldn't she have had fun with me? Why Kunal? Chirag did not say the words which came to his mind. Not keen to share the information that Shreya was probably in trouble, Chirag signed off, saying, "Thanks for telling me, Aadhi. Will you ask Shreya to give me a ping when you see her? Thanks. Goodnight." He disconnected the call immediately.

Turning to Nishaan, he repeated everything Aadhira had told him. "Why the hell did she have to go out with this Kunal? I could have taken her out partying," he grumbled, punching a fist against the seat in front of him.

Noticing the worry on his face, Nishaan placed a pacifying hand on Chirag's shoulder. "We are almost there." He didn't point out to Chirag that he was being unreasonable. After all, hadn't he ignored Shreya royally the whole of yesterday, after kissing her senseless the earlier day?

10

Shreya was happy to go out to a party with Kunal. Being gregarious by nature, and not lacking in self-confidence, she enjoyed meeting new people. And right now, she needed all the distraction she could get, to stop thinking about Chirag during all her waking hours, and dreaming about him while asleep.

The man was too damn handsome and intelligent for words. As for his lovemaking tactics, while she had no way of comparing him with anyone else, she could make out he was an expert. If not a pro, he definitely knew how to make her blood sizzle and her nerves tingle. She had made it clear to him that she wanted to make love with him. Only for him to ignore her over the next thirty-six hours. And after that, he had called to cancel their swimming date. Which could mean only one thing: he wasn't interested in making love to her.

While Shreya had known she was going to feel disappointed if he said no, she hadn't expected to feel so dejected and heartbroken at his rejection.

Her mother's bridegroom hunting plan had served to keep her mind occupied. Shreya had never expected to feel grateful for one such meeting organised by Ambika. But today, she was. Also the reason why she accepted

Kunal's invite to the evening party. While the distraction was something she needed right now, she had also agreed to go out with him mainly because her mother had lost interest in the alliance, once Ambika realised how young Kunal was.

Even now, Ambika made her disapproval clear when Shreya decided to go out with Kunal. "But why, Shreya? It's not as if you both are going to get married. Unless, you aren't telling me something." Ambika gave her daughter a wary glance, a mite worried Shreya was maybe interested in the most unsuitable Kunal Choksi.

Shreya laughed at her mother. "Don't be ridiculous, Mom. Should I meet any man only with marriage in mind? Can't I simply have a fun evening? Kunal isn't interested in marrying me either…"

"Then why has he invited you to go out with him?" wailed Ambika, a worried frown drawing her finely arched eyebrows to meet in the middle of her forehead.

"For the same reason I told you earlier. Why should he meet any woman with only the thought of marriage in mind? We are both going to a party at his friend's house, just to have fun, okay? He has promised to bring me back home."

"Are you sure?"

Shreya reached over to hug her mother. "Of course, Mom. He's a nice guy. No, no. Don't get me wrong. What I mean is, he's a good friend. And I'll try not to be very late, okay?"

Ambika gave her daughter a reluctant nod. She couldn't argue with Shreya's logic, but that didn't stop her from worrying. After all, Delhi wasn't the safest city in the world.

Now, Shreya entered the living room of the low-slung bungalow, not surprised by the loud and pulsating music which thrummed from the many speakers set around the room. While the room was large, it seemed to be full of people, all youngsters. She didn't think there was a single person there, over the age of thirty. And they were all drunk, some of them swaying on their feet. There were many couples who were wrapped around each other, in different stages of nudity. She could see all this through a smoky haze. Shreya scrunched up her nose, not really sure if this was the kind of party she wanted to attend. But well, she was here, and she planned to make the most of it.

"Come, the bar is over there." Kunal took her hand and pulled her along with him, lifting a hand to wave to the people he knew. Well, he couldn't have really spoken to any of them as there was no way anyone could hear themselves even think, not in this kind of noise.

Have I become too old for this? Shreya thought for a moment, and concluded the next instant this simply wasn't her scene.

"What's your poison?" asked Kunal, shouting the words into her ear.

"Beer. I prefer a can if you have it," she shouted to the bartender in turn.

The bartender gave her a leery grin, making Shreya regret the short, sleeveless dress she was wearing. And it was a brilliant red in colour, for God's sake. Had she been mad? But then, she had only wanted to cheer herself up, which the colour tended to do, every time she wore something in red.

"Here!" He handed her the can, after opening it.

Shreya stared at it, a sudden thought forming in her mind as she wondered if it was safe to drink from it. She paused for a moment before placing the open beer can on the counter. "Give me an unopened can," she told him firmly.

"Eh?" Kunal turned around to give her an amused glance. "Why?"

Shreya shrugged. She had heard a lot of stories about substances mixed into drinks, so surreptitiously, the party goers not realising until they were stoned. And this did seem to be that kind of a party. Everyone seemed to be flying higher than a kite. "Just," she said, when she realised he was waiting for an answer.

The bartender's leer turned into a glower as he stared her down, or tried to. Shreya had no qualms about meeting his angry gaze head on, her own eyes completely calm. She crossed her arms across her chest and continued to gaze at him, willing him to give her exactly what she demanded.

"Go on, buddy. Give the lady what she's asking for," said Kunal, rolling his eyes to the ceiling. Turning to Shreya, he asked, "Don't you know how to have fun?"

Taking the unopened beer can the bartender placed on the counter with a thud, she opened it to drink from it before responding to Kunal. "Maybe I don't." She didn't really care what he thought of her, as Shreya decided she didn't like the man, not at all. This was a rave party. She was sure of that. How could he bring her here, without being upfront about it? Shouldn't it have been her decision to attend the party, or not, after knowing all the facts?

"Wanna dance?" asked Kunal, realising he had angered her and making an effort to calm her down. He swore to himself he was going to drug her before the evening was out. It was all in fun. And Kunal took it as his life's challenge, introducing newbies to drugs.

"Not really. I'm famished, actually. Which way is the food?" She turned this way and that to search.

"There." Kunal pointed to their left, where a long table was groaning under the weight of food.

"Awesome." Shreya quickly walked in the direction of the buffet, turning to her left and right to avoid the jostling and sweaty bodies. She winced each time she met the blank gaze of someone who was too high to realise where they were going.

Kunal took a plate to fill it with multiple snacks—*chicken tikka, mutton galouti kabab*, pepper prawns and more. When Shreya took an empty plate in her hand, he said, "Hey, this is all for you. I only plan to get drunk for now."

"Oh, thanks, but no. I am vegetarian," said Shreya, giving him a smile, filling the empty plate in her hand with *hara bara kabab* and *paneer achari*, adding a choice of colourful chutneys to it. Forking a piece of *paneer* into her mouth, she relished it, glad to find the food was damn good. "You go on and enjoy yourself. I'll join you once I finish this lot," she told Kunal.

"Alright." He stepped away from her, though he continued to watch Shreya as she went to sit in one of the chairs which were lined up close to the wall.

Shreya munched her way through the snacks, savouring each bite as she ate slowly, drinking from her beer from time to time. Studying the people in front of her, she didn't notice Kunal watching her avidly from the other side of the room.

Sometime later, Kunal carried a plate with a choice of four different pastries in it. "Do you have a sweet tooth?" he tempted her, a charming smile on his face.

Shreya gave him a wide smile, happy now on her full stomach. "How did you guess? Are all of these for me?" she asked, eyeing the cakes greedily. Picking up the blueberry cheesecake, she popped it into her mouth, closing her eyes to relish it all the more. "Mmm… this is so damn good. Thanks, Kunal."

"My pleasure." Kunal had an extremely pleased expression on his face. After all, he had drizzled all four pastries with the white powder he always carried in his pocket.

Licking her fingers clean, Shreya reached out for the chocolate cake and ate it too. She truly liked the bite-sized pieces they served here. The caterer was obviously high-end, she thought to herself. "You wanna have one?" Shreya offered the plate to Kunal. She dropped the plate into her lap when she felt a sudden buzz in her head, her eyesight blurring for a second. Squinting her eyes, she scowled deeply, trying to check out the area around her. Glad to find everything appearing clear, she decided she must have probably imagined it. Taking the plate in her hand once again, she offered it to Kunal. "Go on, take one. Or there won't be anything left for you in a few minutes." She laughed out loud, before clapping her hand over her mouth. What the hell was wrong with her? It wasn't as if she wasn't used to laughing loudly. But somehow, her laugh today sounded extra loud, as if she was high.

High! Oh my God! "Kunal? What's in the cake?" The buzz she had earlier felt in her head, suddenly became louder, while sparks seemed to fly in front of her gaze, little star bursts which made her feel dizzy.

Kunal gave her a broad grin, reaching over to take the piece of strawberry shortcake and popping it into his mouth. He munched on it, continuing to eye her with amusement.

"Kunal? Have you drugged me?"

"Eh? Drugged you is kind of strong. Tell me something. Have you never tried imbibing marijuana or coke or something like that?"

Shreya shook her head before holding it with both her hands when the dizziness increased. "Of course not," she said, trying to glare at him and failing miserably.

He shrugged. "What's with the "of course not"?" Kunal asked, drawing two quotation marks in the air with the fingers of both his hands. "You drink beer, don't you? Probably whisky too?"

"So?" It was difficult but she kept her brown gaze focused on him.

"Then why not coke? Which is what I sprinkled on the cakes. Yummy, weren't they?"

"You're a bastard, Kunal. I…"

Kunal shook his head, continuing to smile. "Don't be silly, Shreya. How can you say that, after meeting both my parents?" He laughed uproariously as if he had cracked an extremely funny joke. "Listen, this is all only in fun. It's not as if this will turn you into an addict. Don't you like the buzz you are feeling in your head? As if you are transformed?" He watched her face eagerly, even as he waited for her to agree with him.

"Go to hell!" Shreya took out her phone to message Chirag. She couldn't think of anyone else who would go to her rescue. And she definitely needed rescuing from this madhouse. After pressing the send button, she simply continued to sit on the chair, ignoring Kunal completely.

Kunal tried talking to her a few times, doing his best to reason with her as he was keen to convince her that imbibing substances was such a harmless exercise. Finally accepting she was simply not interested, he walked away from her to join his friends in their merrymaking.

It was about an hour later when Chirag and Nishaan arrived at the bungalow, walking in as if they owned the place. They stopped in their tracks when they saw there were at least seventy to eighty people in the front room, in various states of inebriation.

Chirag went pale when he noticed the smoke wafting over the dimly lit room. Where the hell had Shreya landed? Alone, too. As far as he was concerned, Kunal Choksi was the villain. He was going to throttle the man the moment he set eyes on him.

"Come with me," said Nishaan, beginning to walk around the periphery of the room, stopping to stare at the women's faces, simply ignoring them when some of the men threatened to dismember him. Oaths and catcalls followed in their wake as the two friends walked along the length of the room.

"There!" Chirag pointed at the bar before rushing forward at a jog. At least, he tried to go as fast as it was possible, pushing his way through all the inebriated dancers.

Nishaan lifted his head to look in the direction his friend was pointing in, and there she was, Shreya. Wearing the shortest dress in the hottest shade of red, her four-inch heels in the same colour, she was on top of the bar, swinging her arms, shaking her hips, and tapping her feet to the thumping music, while a crowd of men clapped loudly, trying to keep pace with the music, and failing badly. But it was obvious from their raucous laughter that they were enjoying themselves. Nishaan rushed right behind Chirag, more because he wasn't keen his friend murdered someone in the jealous temper he was so obviously in.

The Sagittarius leaped forward like the centaur he was, pushing at the men surrounding her with both his hands, before striding forth to stand at the bar. He wrapped his large hands around Shreya's slim waist, effectively stopping her from dancing, much to her audience's annoyance.

"Chiraaaaag! You came." Shreya squealed in delight as she threw herself against him, wrapping both her arms and legs tightly around his lithe body. Pressing her pouting mouth to his manly lips in a brief kiss, she declared loudly, "My hero!"

Refusing to be pacified by her fervent greeting—after all, he had been so sure she had been enjoying herself too much to be interested in his arrival—he tightened his arms around her before turning away from the bar.

"Where do you think you're going with my girlfriend?" Kunal stepped in front of Chirag, unmoved by the fact that the other man was at least four inches taller than he was. "And who the hell are you?"

"Get out of my way. Unless you want me to break your nose," snarled Chirag, concluding that the guy who was standing in front of him must be Kunal Choksi, the one who had brought Shreya to this rave party, the bastard!

Placing his hands on his hips, Kunal stood his ground, his legs spread apart in a fighting stance. "Go on and try, if you want," he said, tilting his head to the side with a smirk on his face.

Nishaan placed a firm hand on Kunal's shoulder and pressed hard, making the younger man feel his strength. "I think it's best you get out of my friend's way," he spoke in a quiet voice.

"And who would you be?"

"Does it really matter?"

"It does, when you both are trying to steal my girlfriend…"

Chirag roared loudly, not letting Kunal finish his sentence. His hands were full, and he had no plans of letting go of Shreya. Should he kick the man instead?

"I'm sure the lady thinks differently," said Nishaan, pointing a thumb at Shreya who was clinging to Chirag as if her whole life depended on it. "See?"

Kunal glared at Nishaan before turning to address Shreya. "Come on, Shreya. You came to the party with me. You can't leave so soon. I…"

Perched in Chirag's arms, Shreya turned around to look down at Kunal's face from her superior height. "Get out of the way, Kunal. I never want to see your ugly face again." Turning right back to Chirag, she said, "Please take me away from here."

Nishaan shoved Kunal out of the way so Chirag could walk down the hall towards the doorway. No one there was really in a state to stop them as they were all under the influence of various drugs and liquor. He opened the back door to the waiting cab so Chirag could place his Shreya on the seat. Opening the passenger door in the front, Nishaan settled his long frame into it.

Chirag pushed Shreya none too gently to the other end of the cab before climbing into the seat next to her. He had a good mind to drag her across his knees and give her the sound thrashing he was sure she deserved.

Refusing to look in her direction, he faced the front, his gaze unseeing as it fell on the back of Nishaan's head, his jaw clenched hard.

"Chirag." Shreya placed a hand on his shoulder, before moving close to his side and leaning her head against his arm. "Thank you," she said, closing her tired eyes. The extreme level of energy which had been fizzing inside her, which had urged her on to dance to the loud music, was all drained out and she felt totally beat. Her day had started early, with her dolling up to go to lunch at the Choksis' residence. They had got home in the late afternoon, only for her to dress up again—at least, this time, she had worn something she liked—and go to the party with Kunal. She truly regretted going with him. Her mother had been right; Kunal was ridiculously young and immature, even for a date. Was she glad she could call on Chirag to help her out of the perilous situation! She had been so sure he would go to her rescue. And why was that, she knew not.

Chirag turned to his side to look at Shreya, a smile tugging at his mouth when he noticed her fast asleep as she clung to his side, her mouth hanging open. Reaching with his left hand, he pushed her small chin up to close her mouth before wrapping his right arm around her slender form. Forgetting all about the driver and his best friend sitting in the front of the cab, he pushed back the hair which had fallen on her forehead to kiss it gently.

Nishaan, who could see the interplay via the rear-view mirror, smiled at his friend's overtures. While he could see Chirag had fallen for young Shreya, hook, line, and sinker, it was also obvious to him that his best friend had no clue about the depth of his own feelings. Nishaan knew, for he had never seen such an expression of tenderness on Chirag's face, ever before.

"Do you want me to wait for you? Or should I go on to my place?" asked Nishaan, once they reached the building Shreya lived in. Well, he wasn't sure how long Chirag planned to be, as he seemed to be on such cosy terms, not only with Shreya, but also her younger sister, Aadhira.

"Aren't you coming up?" asked Chirag, getting out of the cab.

"Of course not, man." Nishaan didn't think Shreya's parents would appreciate him arriving at their doorstep, not after the way their bridegroom hunting of the Ahuja scion had fallen by the wayside.

Walking to the other side of the cab to pull Shreya out, Chirag said, "Wait for me right here. I'll be back ASAP."

"Fine." Nishaan gave him a nod before stepping out of the cab to call his fiancée.

"Shrey, wake up. We've reached." Chirag shook her shoulder gently even as he pulled her out of the cab.

"Mmm…" Shreya slid along the seat and directly into his arms, without bothering to open her eyes.

"Shrey?" Chirag stood her next to the cab, shaking her shoulder once again.

"Mmm… sleepy," she slurred, leaning against his chest, her arms hanging at her sides.

Realising she wasn't going to wake up any time soon, Chirag lifted her into his arms and threw her over his shoulder as he walked to the gate of her building. She felt so light, weighing so little. Chirag felt a wave of tenderness wash over him as he lifted a hand to the security guard, to open the small door set in the gate for people to walk through.

Recognising Shreya Udhas from the tenth floor, the security guard opened the door to let the man inside. "Do you need help, sir?"

"If you could call for the lift, please?" Chirag followed the guard to the elevator and was glad when it came almost immediately. "Thanks, man," he said, before pushing the button for the tenth floor, having got the full address from Aadhira. He let Shreya down to stand in front of him, his arm wrapped around her to make sure she didn't fall down. He looked at her face, not really surprised to see she was out like the light. She had obviously been drugged by that idiotic Choksi fellow. He called Aadhira once he was out of the lift, not keen to ring the doorbell as it was almost midnight. He didn't want Shreya's father to shoot him dead.

The door opened almost immediately. "Hey," said Aadhira, giving him a smile, which disappeared the moment she noticed Shreya. "Why are you carrying her over your shoulder?" she asked him in a panic-stricken whisper.

"Are your parents awake?" Chirag responded with a whispered question of his own.

"Nope. Come along in."

"Phew!" He quickly followed her, after sliding his feet out of his leather moccasins, his bare feet making no sound as he walked along the hallway towards the door which was the furthest from the entrance.

Aadhira pushed the door open to the bedroom she shared with Shreya. "Come on inside," she invited, pointing a finger towards the single bed which was against the opposite wall. "That one is Shreya's," she added in the way of explanation. She had no qualms closing the bedroom door silently as she watched Chirag placing her sister gently on the bed, before removing her red heels. "What happened?"

Chirag turned to Aadhira, after covering Shreya with the comforter. "Hello," he said, giving her a smile, "we finally meet."

Aadhira gave him a shy smile, understanding why her sister had fallen for the man. For one thing, he was too damn handsome for words. For another, she hadn't missed the way he had carried Shreya, as if she was the most precious person in the whole world. "Hi," she responded, "Yes."

"I'd better leave," he said, stepping towards the door.

"But you haven't told me what happened to Shrey."

Chirag stopped in his tracks to glance back at Aadhira's face. She was obviously younger than Shreya and was probably still a teenager. "I think she's just too tired from a hectic day," he said.

"But she went out with Kunal Choksi. How come you ended up bringing her home?"

Chirag turned around fully to face the young lady, giving her a reassuring smile. "She asked me to bring her home as Kunal intended to remain there for much longer. Oh, and by the way, Shrey might wake up with a headache. She needs to be well hydrated. Will you take care?" he asked, reaching over to give Aadhira an affectionate pat on her round cheek.

Aadhira gave him a wide smile. "Of course. And thank you, Chirag, for bringing my sister home safely."

"Not at all. I'll let myself out. Goodnight."

"Let me come with you, just in case someone wakes up." Aadhira went along with him, waving him off once he stepped outside the front door.

Shreya woke up with a groan, her head pounding as if someone was striking it with a hammer relentlessly.

"Good morning," said Aadhira in her most cheerful voice. "Here you go," she said, offering her sister a bottle of water.

"Is there a need to be so cheerful this early in the morning?" moaned Shreya, drinking the water in desperate gulps.

Aadhira laughed, reaching over to grab the half empty bottle from Shreya's hand, bothered that her sister might choke. She had read somewhere that drinking too much water on a dehydrated stomach might not be all that good.

"Give it back to me," ordered Shreya, trying to grab the bottle back, annoyed when Aadhira held it out of her reach. "What are you playing at, Aadhi? Do you want me to die of thirst?" Shreya tried to glare at her sister, but ended up squinting instead. "And why have you opened the curtains? It's so damn bright in here."

"Complaint master," accused Aadhira, keeping the bottle aside to give Shreya a mock glare. "What had you been up to last night?"

"It's none of your business," grumbled Shreya, pissed with her sister. She tried to sit up, only to fall back on her pillows with a loud groan. "Give me the water," she told her sister in a scolding voice.

"Let me get you the perfect antidote for your hangover. And stay away from the water until I return," said Aadhira, walking out of the room without a backward glance.

Shreya didn't think she had the energy to go and get the water bottle herself. She held her head in both her hands, taking deep breaths to stop herself from throwing up. What the hell had Kunal given her? Bastard! She frowned deeply, trying—without any success—to recall reaching home the earlier night, and getting into bed. That was when she noticed she was still wearing the red dress she had worn to the party. How had she got back home? She frowned at Aadhira when she returned to the room with a steaming mug. "How did I get home yesterday?"

"Don't you remember anything?" asked Aadhira, a naughty smile on her face. "But first, drink this," she said, offering the mug to Shreya.

"What's it?" asked Shreya, giving her sister a suspicious glance as she accepted the mug. But the aroma from the lemon and ginger tea made her feel a tad better and she took a small sip from the mug. She moaned in delight as she relished the taste of just the right amount of salt and honey added to the concoction. "Thanks, Aadhi," she said, giving her sister a grateful smile.

"You're welcome, sis," said Aadhira, sitting next to Shreya on her bed. "Don't you recall anything?" she asked.

"Of course not. I mean, of course I remember going to the party with Kunal. I…" she paused. "What time is it?"

"Shouldn't you be asking what day it is?" asked Aadhira, an impish smile on her face.

"No!" Shreya was horrified. "You're pulling my leg. It must be Sunday."

Aadhira lifted both her hands in front of her in a gesture of peace. "Sorry, couldn't resist. It's Sunday, ten am."

"Ouch! What have you told Mom and Dad?" asked Shreya, a scowl forming on her forehead.

"Just that you were late returning home and were still sleeping."

"How did you manage to get the tea?" asked Shreya, continuing to frown as she took a few more sips, her head already feeling a tad better for it.

"I made it for everyone, telling them I was trying out a new recipe I found on YouTube," said Aadhira, laughing.

Shreya reached across to kiss her sister's cheek. "Thanks, Aadhi. You're a life saver."

"What happened at the party?"

Shreya gave a loud sigh, which didn't seem to have any effect on her sister; at least, nothing like what she expected. Realising she didn't have much of a choice, she declared, "That Kunal is a bastard. He drugged me."

"What?" Aadhira jumped to her feet to stare at Shreya with wide eyes the size of saucers, her hands clamped one over the other across her mouth. "Don't tell me!"

"I realised what kind of a party it was the moment I went inside the bungalow. I insisted the bartender gave me an unopened can of beer. Oh yes," she said, stopping

Aadhira from asking the question which was on the tip of her tongue. "He did try to give me an opened can, but I refused. I thought I was being smart, but in the end, Kunal spiked the dessert. The cakes were so damn delicious and I had… three of those, I think."

"Oh my God! Then?"

"My head began to spin and I realised what must have happened. Kunal didn't even bother to deny it when I asked him. He seems to think taking drugs is a part and parcel of everyday life."

"What a rogue! Then?"

"I quickly sent a message to Chirag, asking him for help. I also managed to send him the location. I was sitting for a while, but some of them dragged me to dance. By then, I was as high as a kite and jumped into the fray."

"When did Chirag reach you?"

A heavy scowl pleated Shreya's forehead. "That's what. I don't remember anything after that. Did Chirag bring me home?" she asked.

Aadhira grinned from ear to ear. "Yes."

"But how did he know where to bring me?" Shreya was totally flummoxed. The last she remembered was when she had climbed up onto the bar. Many of the revellers at the party had been clapping to the rhythm of the music and she had… danced. Oh yes! She recalled dancing on the bar. But… what had happened after that?

"Isn't it a good thing Chirag knows my number and called me?" asked Aadhira, giving her sister a cheeky smile.

"What? How?"

"Later. I think it's best if you have a shower and get some hot breakfast inside you," said Aadhira, firmly. "Doctor's orders!" she added.

"Who do you mean?"

"Okay! If you want to know, those are Chirag's orders."

"Who the hell is he to order me about?" grumbled Shreya, getting out of the bed. She held her head for a few moments when she felt it take a slow spin. "Okay, I'll do what he says, this one time."

"Phew!" said Aadhira, at her dramatic best. She messaged Chirag the moment Shreya went into the bathroom. "All good, Chirag. Shrey's up and has gone for a shower. I think the ginger and lemon tea worked well. I'll be in touch."

"Good to know. Thanks for keeping me updated, Aadhi," came the prompt response.

"Shreya, finally! Why are you so late?" asked Ambika, not missing the dark circles under her daughter's eyes. Her main worry was how Shreya's outing with Kunal had gone. What in case her daughter decided to consider him as a prospective husband? Ambika shuddered at the thought.

Aadhira smartly hid herself away in her bedroom, not wanting to be a party to the question-and-answer session she was sure her mother was planning with her elder sister.

"Good morning, Mom," responded Shreya. "Where's Dad?" She had been hoping Sunil would be home to help her deflect her mother's questions. "Where are Aryan and Sumit for that matter?" she asked, hoping against hope her mother wasn't going to ask any awkward questions.

Tina stepped out of the kitchen to place a steaming plate of *khaman dhokla* along with green chutney in front of her. "Do you want tea or coffee?" asked the cook.

"Thank you, Tina *di*. You are the best," said Shreya, her stomach growling in hunger. "I think I'll have *masala chai*."

"Good." Tina returned to the kitchen to make fresh tea with ginger and the special *masala* she prepared on a daily basis, consisting of cloves, cinnamon and cardamom.

"Tea? You want to have tea?" asked Ambika, her eyes going so wide they were on the verge of popping out of her forehead. As far as she knew, Shreya was a coffee fanatic. She never, but never, had tea. What was different today? Was this Kunal a tea-drinker? Had he already influenced her daughter? The mother's mind ran around in circles.

"Yes, Mom. Do you mind?" While Shreya's pounding head had calmed down, there was still a dull ache. How she wished her mother would remain quiet! But she couldn't really blame Ambika who appeared anxious all of a sudden. And Shreya could sense the reason for it. If only she hadn't gone out with Kunal the earlier evening! Tch! But then, it was all because of Chirag. She placed all the blame on his handsome head. How could he have ignored her after the way they had kissed each other on Thursday evening? But then, according to Aadhira, Chirag was the one who had gone to her rescue last night. Beyond messaging him her location, Shreya had no recall of any contact with the man.

"But why?" asked Ambika, "You always drink coffee."

"That's right, Mom. But I feel like having tea today. Is there a problem?" asked Shreya, eating her way through the spongy *dhoklas*, enjoying every bite. She was glad her appetite wasn't impaired by her adventures of the earlier night.

"When did you get home last night? Did Kunal drop you?" Ambika was dying to ask Shreya about her outing with the boy.

Shreya stopped eating to look at her mother, not missing the anxiety on her face. "Mom." She placed a hand over her mother's as it lay on the dining table. "If you are worried about my interest in Kunal, you can stop right now. He is too damn young, exactly as you said. I just wanted to go to a party. He invited and I accepted. That's all there is to it. And I returned at around midnight. And no, it wasn't Kunal who dropped me. But a couple of my friends who were also there at the party."

"Who are these friends?" Ideally, Ambika should have been satisfied when her daughter told her she wasn't interested in Kunal Choksi. But the mother's curiosity was piqued.

"It was Nishaan Ahuja and his girlfriend." Shreya lied through her teeth as she met her mother's piercing gaze boldly.

"Oh!"

It was an effort for Chirag to stop himself from rushing over to Shreya's house to check on her. That way lay danger, just as Shreya had warned him. What if Shreya's mother pressurised her into considering Chirag as a prospective bridegroom? Which was the reason he curbed his impulse and stayed put at home, glad for the distraction from Jack and Jill.

It was a good thing Shreya's sister Aadhira kept him updated about the situation, or he might have climbed the wall in frustration.

As for Shreya, he supposed she was still not fully recovered from her adventure of the earlier night. It was thanks to Nishaan's calming influence that Kunal Choksi didn't have a broken nose and blackened eyes. Though the bastard deserved no less. How dare he take Shreya to a rave party of all places? Stupid moron!

It was an hour later when his phone pinged again. "Thank you." It was a bald message from Shreya. Grr! *My foot!*

On the verge of responding to her message, he changed his mind to call her, dying to hear her voice; glad when she took his call immediately. "Hi Shrey."

"Hello." Shreya's voice was hoarse, with longing more than the aftermath of a drug induced sleep. She wanted to see him, needed his arms around her, and his mouth on hers. "Chirag…" His name was a sigh on her lips.

"What's it, sweetheart?" He didn't miss the yearning in her voice as she uttered his name, his body aching with the need to hold her in his arms before exploring every inch of her soft and silky skin. *Will she let me make love to her?*

"I want to see you," said Shreya, her anger towards him melting away on hearing his voice.

"Should I pick you up?" he asked, getting up from where he had been lounging on the sofa, idly surfing the channels on TV.

"Tell me where to meet you," she said. This time, she meant business. She planned to seduce him, if it came to that.

"Let me send you the address to my apartment. And Shrey?"

"Mmm."

"I'm dying to hold you in my arms." He made his intentions clear.

Shreya's heart soared even as a wide smile spread over her tired face. "Oh, yes, please. I'll see you soon." She booked an Uber the moment she received the address to his bachelor pad, her heart thumping loudly in her chest, and left soon after. She pressed her cold hands against her hot cheeks, doing her best to balance her temperature, but she was simply too excited about her upcoming rendezvous with the handsome and sexy Chirag Bhatia.

Would he only kiss her this time? Or give in to his urges and make love to her fully? *Well, I will have to just convince him, don't I?* The bold Aquarius woman decided to simply follow her instincts.

"Hey, where are you?" Chirag called Shreya to find out some time later.

"Google Map says five minutes," she said, her voice hoarse with excitement. "Have you reached?" she asked.

"Just. And Shrey? I can't wait to kiss you."

A soft laugh escaped her throat before a goofy grin spread over her face as Shreya clutched the phone to her ear. "I can't either," she responded in a whisper.

"You can't what?" he asked, a smile in his voice. He was sure she wouldn't be able to answer him honestly, not with a driver within hearing distance, sitting in the front seat of the cab.

"Let me come and tell you."

"Now? Please?" His voice was husky with desire as he imagined her sitting in the back of the cab, leaning against the window while she chatted with him on the phone.

"Just a sec." Shreya stepped out of the cab, paying the fare via GPay. "Just watch it, Chirag. I'm going to kiss you senseless," she declared.

"Ooh! I can't wait," he said, his whole body growing hard with need. "I presume you've got out of the cab?" He walked out of his ground floor apartment and watched her stepping into the compound. "Here!" he called out, lifting a hand to grab her attention.

Shreya cut the call when her eyes fell on Chirag, admiring the handsome figure he cut in dark blue jeans and a black t-shirt, his large feet thrust into rubber slippers. "Hello," she said, climbing up the few steps which led to the entrance of his flat.

His dark eyes lit up when they fell on her slender figure clad in a pair of knee length denim dungarees, coupled with a t-shirt in soft pink. "Hello, sweetheart." He grabbed her with both arms before carrying her into his flat and kicking the door shut with his foot.

"Chirag!" Shreya gasped in protest, grabbing his neck for support. "Don't you find me heavy?" she asked, looking into his sinfully black gaze, colour rushing into her cheeks when she noticed the heat in it.

"Now she asks me," said Chirag, rolling his eyes to the ceiling and back to her beautiful face. "Don't you remember how I carried you back to your home last night?"

Her eyes went wide in astonishment. "You carried me all the way?"

"Of course. How else could I have got you home? You were completely knocked out."

She grimaced. "I simply presumed you must have walked me…"

"Hahaha! That would have been impractical." He reached over to nuzzle her neck. "You smell so awesome. Let me see, roses?"

"Mmm…" She tilted her neck to accommodate him, sighing deeply when he nipped her skin before soothing it with the tip of his tongue.

She tasted so damn good! And went to his head like a powerful aphrodisiac. He continued to nibble along her jaw, making his way towards her ear, even as he let her slide down to stand in the circle of his arms, her lush body pressed to his muscular one.

Shreya clutched his head with eager hands, her fingers sliding through the silky black strands, even as she turned this way and that to capture his foraging mouth.

She made a sound of frustration when he continued to tease her with his nips and strokes along her jaw as he proceeded to the other side of her neck. "Chirag!" she protested.

Lifting his face to look down at her, he asked, "What?" A wicked black eyebrow rose up in query as he ran his dark gaze over her flushed face. His hands were busy unbuttoning the straps of her dungarees before pushing them down her arms.

Meeting his gaze boldly, she went on her toes to press her mouth to his, tracing the shape of his masculine lips with the tip of her tongue.

Chirag groaned loudly, opening his mouth to capture hers in a hot and torrid kiss which made him feel shaky at the knees. Without letting go of her mouth, he lifted her once again in his arms to carry her over to the bedroom. Standing her next to the bed, he asked, "Are you sure?" He was going to die of frustration if she refused him now.

Shreya met his hot gaze head on, her honey brown eyes shimmering with excitement. Taking his hand, she placed it over her left breast. "Can you feel my heart pumping at double pace? It's for you," she declared. "We have all the privacy we need here. You cannot escape from making love to me, Chirag."

He relaxed completely, his face lighting up with a lazy grin. She wanted him, as much as he wanted her. He cupped her left breast and kneaded it gently, grinning some more when he heard her gasp of pleasure. "Your heart is beating hardcrazily," he agreed, looking deeply into her eyes. Lifting his other hand, he cupped her right breast and squeezed it too, his breath hitching when he felt the hard nubs push against his palms through her thin t-shirt, thrilled to note she wore no bra. One less barrier to overcome!

"Show me how to please you," she managed to gasp even as she pressed her upper body into his caressing hands. No, she didn't wear a bra, unable to stand its scrape on her sensitive breasts every time she visualised his hands on them; which is what she had been doing all the way to his bachelor pad.

Leaning down to kiss her mouth, he spoke against her lips. "You please me just as you are."

She took his lower lip between her teeth and nibbled on it, loving the sensation, before stroking the area with her tongue.

"Shrey… sweetheart." He pulled her lower body closer to his, groaning when he felt her soft abdomen fit snugly against his hardened shaft.

Shreya felt it too, his manhood pulsing against her stomach. It excited her no end. She pulled his t-shirt out of the waistband of his jeans, running her hands eagerly over the bare skin of his lean waist.

Chirag took a step back, smiling when he heard her mewl of protest. "Patience, sweetheart," he told her in a hoarse voice, pulling his t-shirt over his head.

Shreya's eyes went wide as she stared at his muscular torso, the light sprinkling of hair only adding to his masculinity. She followed the line as it disappeared into his jeans, a hot blush colouring her face when she noticed the bulge pushing against his fly.

He stood there in front of her, proud as a peacock, ignoring the tightening of his body as he felt the warmth of her shy gaze checking him out. "Like what you see?" he asked, his voice a gentle and teasing whisper.

She lifted her gaze up to meet his, the colour on her cheeks only deepening when she noticed the heat and desire in his coal black eyes. "So far, so good. But you'll have to wait until I can check you out fully," she told him boldly, a small grin splitting her features when she heard his startled shout of laughter.

Shaking his head at her, Chirag continued with his striptease, a first for him as he unbuckled the leather belt, before snapping open the metal button at the waist of his jeans. The sound of the zipper being pulled open filled the silent room, as he continued to pin her gaze with his.

It was an effort for Shreya to break her eye connection with his as her curiosity drove her to look down at his lower body which was becoming visible to her, inch by torturous inch as he drew his jeans slowly down the length of his powerful thighs, and then to his knees before letting them fall at his feet. Stepping out of them, he kicked the jeans out of the way before standing tall in front of her once again.

Saliva pooled in Shreya's mouth as she slid her eyes up the length of the magnificent specimen of manhood in front of her, her gaze slowly rising from his broad feet all the way up to meet his steamy gaze once again.

Crossing his muscular arms against his chest, "Your turn," he invited, lifting a challenging eyebrow at her.

Shreya licked her dry lips as she continued to stare at him, aghast. Did he expect her to do a strip show for him? Really? The colour which had surged up her face earlier, slowly drained out, leaving it a pale oval. Her eyes appeared like large brown saucers as she gaped at him. It wouldn't be so difficult if he had been holding her against his damn sexy body. But with the distance of a couple of feet between them, it seemed kind of clinical to someone who had never done this before.

"Sweetheart?" Chirag stepped closer to Shreya. "I can help you," he offered, his voice hoarse with desire as he thrust his large hands inside her dungarees before pushing them down her slender hips, revelling in the texture of her silky skin as he ran them down the sides of her thighs and calves as he took the garment all the way down to her feet.

Shreya placed her hands on his shoulders for purchase, her eyes shut tightly as she savoured his touch on her sensitised skin, her pulse leaping in response. She lifted her feet one by one as he drew her dungarees completely off her before throwing the garment over his shoulder.

Chirag got up in one fluid movement, his hands clutching the hem of her pastel pink t-shirt with the print of Bugs Bunny at the front. "Cute," he commented, touching one floppy ear with the tip of his finger. "May I?" he asked, waiting for her to open her eyes to look at him.

"What?" she asked, giving him a confused look.

He simply drew the t-shirt up her naked body, his breath catching in his throat when his gaze fell on her plump breasts. God! She was gorgeous. Throwing her t-shirt also over his shoulder, he flicked the tip of her left breast with his forefinger.

Shreya moaned, her eyes shutting automatically, to better savour the sensation of his roaming hands on her body, while her mouth fell open in awe.

A smile of triumph lit his face when her nipple pebbled up right in front of his gaze. Stroking it with his thumb, he turned to pay his attention to her right breast, fascinated when he noticed the other tip had also become rigid, even before he could touch it. Leaning down, he drew the tip of his tongue over the nub, his shaft tightening painfully when he heard her needy moan. His right hand squeezing her left breast, Chirag closed his mouth over the tip he had been caressing with his tongue and drew on it gently at first, before suckling greedily. He was down on his knees by now as he played with her breasts, his teeth grazing the tips in turn.

She clutched his head in her hands, thrusting her upper body as close to him as it was humanly possible, completely unaware of the mewling noises emanating from her throat. She felt treasured by his lovemaking and never wanted him to stop. She relished every moment he fed on her breasts as if he was satiating the hunger of a million years. "Sss…" she moaned when he took another bite of the plump flesh above her nipple, leaving his mark on her.

"Did I hurt you?" There was regret in the black eyes which looked up at her apologetically. "I'm sorry…"

She placed her hand on his mouth, shaking her head from side to side, her long, silky hair fluffing out over her shoulders, a couple of strands landing on his face. "No, no. Don't stop now, Chirag. I'm loving it too much." She cupped a hand below her breast and offered it to him, watching in fascination when he drew the nipple into his mouth, his eyes fixed on hers. "More," she demanded in a hoarse voice, colouring heavily when he took more of her flesh into his mouth. "Yeaaaaahhhh!!" she moaned, her head falling back. Feeling her knees quivering, she lifted a leg to drape it over his shoulder, sighing with relief when she felt confident she wouldn't fall down now.

He clutched her hip, moving closer between her legs as he continued to make love to her breasts. She was insatiable and he simply adored that about her. It was a long while before he let go of her breasts to kiss his way down, nibbling on the skin stretched over her ribs. He paused when she giggled, lifting his head to look up at her.

Shaking her head at him, "I'm ticklish there," she said.

A naughty grin split his face as he poked a finger over the second last rib on her right side. "There?"

Shreya giggled some more, her whole body quivering with mirth. "No, Chirag, stop. You're killing me."

Laughing softly, he kissed the spot gently before moving lower.

Her breath caught in her throat when she felt his tongue exploring her navel, even as he caressed both her legs from hip to ankle with his large, manly hands. His warm breath heated up her abdomen, rousing her to fever pitch. "Chirag…?"

"Hmm?" He lifted his face once again to look up at her.

"I need the bed. My legs won't hold up much longer." She spoke in a whisper, her left hand holding the back of his head, while her right hand clutched his left shoulder.

"Oh yes!" Removing her leg from his shoulder, he rose to his feet before lifting her up into his arms.

"How do you do it?" she asked, giving him a wondrous glance. "My body is so fluid, ready to pool down right here on the floor."

He gave her a cocky grin. "A man's muscle is built differently, I suppose."

"My ass," she said, giving him a saucy look and was rewarded with a pinch on her bottom, which made her yelp. Rubbing her hand over the area he had pinched, she gave him a mock glare. "That hurt, you brute!"

"Here, let me kiss it right," he offered, rolling her to her front on the bed before drawing her lacy panties down her legs. He went on his knees beside her on the bed, a large hand on her small of her back as he held her down. Leaning down, he kissed her curvaceous bottom; open mouthed kisses which drove her crazy with pleasure.

She clutched the bed sheet with both her fists, her buttocks on fire under the onslaught of his teeth and tongue. *Did buttocks have nerves in them?* That question was for another day, thought Shreya as she felt him slide a finger between her bottom to reach her vagina. A loud gasp escaped her throat when she felt him exploring the most private part of her body. "Chirag?" her voice was a trembling whisper as she turned her head to the side, calling out to him.

"Sweetheart." He pushed his middle finger deep inside her core, smiling when he found it satisfyingly wet. Removing his hand to give her a hard pat on her bottom, he rolled her over to face him. Unable to resist, he cupped his hand over her feminine mound, his watchful eyes on hers, checking for any signs of discomfort.

Shreya sighed, moving her legs apart to accommodate his large, caressing hand. *Oh, he was good,* she thought, thrusting her lower body against his hand, moaning when she felt his fingers—two of them now—pushing and pulling from within her.

"Come on, sweetheart," he invited softly, "come for me," as he increased the speed of his thrusting fingers.

Her moans became louder as she felt the clench deep inside her womb, the waves building up relentlessly, growing bigger and bigger, before they broke over the banks to flow unheeded. A long and loud moan made its way out of her throat, her body stretched upward, taut as a bow, before Shreya fell back on the bed, completely spent, her chest heaving as she tried to gain the breath which she seemed to have lost.

Chirag moved up on the bed to lie down next to her, holding her close against his chest, a triumphant smile on his face.

Turning on her side to face him, she buried her face in the crook of his shoulder, snuggling deeply into his arms. "What did you do to me?" she asked after a long time, once she was sure she could breathe normally again.

"What do you think I did to you?" he asked her right back, smiling into her eyes.

"I climaxed…"

"And how!" he exclaimed, lifting a cocky eyebrow at her. "Your first?" he asked, confident of himself.

"Mmm." A soft blush illumined her cheeks as she continued to look into his eyes. "But you didn't… you didn't really participate in the act…" She hesitated, awkward with the unfamiliar words.

He threw back his head and laughed out loud, not noticing the frown which gathered on her forehead.

"Are you laughing at me?" she asked outright, pushing away from him to lie at the furthest edge of the bed.

He shook his head, unable to stop grinning. "Never! You are so damn innocent that I…" He paused, his heavy eyelids sliding closed in a half slit as he gazed at her adorable face. What had he been going to say? *I'm falling for you…* NO! Of course not! He turned away from her to lie down on his back, shocked to the depth of his core. How can that be possible? He had known her for less than a week. And he didn't do permanent, never. As if 'never' wasn't permanent in itself. But Chirag wasn't feeling logical right now. Anything but!

Thoroughly miffed, Shreya got out of the bed, ignoring her trembling legs as she walked towards the attached bathroom. Being what she was, she didn't feel awkward about her nakedness, not noticing the way his eyes were following her avidly, while she was steeped in her own misery. She washed herself quickly, glad for the hot water, taking the towel on the rack to dry herself. She checked her face in the mirror, not missing the way her mouth was: relaxed. Despite what she had undergone last night. And the strain and dark circles around her eyes had completely disappeared. Could sex do that to a person? But then, what she had experienced was not exactly sex, was it? She had had an orgasm, thanks to Chirag's clever fingers. She blushed as she recalled the way he had administered to her so selflessly. Then why was she angry with him?

A knock sounded on the bathroom door just as she was going to step out. Opening it immediately, she faced Chirag boldly.

"Are you okay?" he asked, a wary expression in his eyes. It was an effort to keep them on hers, as they wanted to slide down her body to stare at the lush twin mounds.

"Ne'er been better," she said, throwing her arms around his neck and clinging to him. "Now will you make proper love to me?" she whispered in his ear, nibbling on the lobe. "I have not even seen you fully," she added, making her meaning clear as she pressed a hand over the front of his briefs.

Chirag groaned as he felt a burst of desire run through his veins, wrapping his arms around her slender body, and smiling when he felt her legs going around his waist. Cupping his hands over her bottom, he turned right about to carry her to the bed.

"I think it's time you got naked," she continued to whisper in his ear.

"I agree," he said, leaning down to place her on the bed and kissing her deeply. Letting her go reluctantly, he stood up to remove his briefs, sighing with relief when his shaft sprang forth as if escaping a trap.

She stared at him, open mouthed, her eyes going wide. "God! You are beautiful!" she exclaimed, reaching over to touch his twitching manhood with the tip of one finger. Laughing softly when he twitched some more in response, she curled her left hand over his member, her thumb caressing the head.

"Are you trying to kill me, sweetheart?" Chirag groaned loudly, colour washing over his slashed cheeks.

"Eh?" Instead of letting go, she gripped him all the tighter as she went on her knees to get closer to him. "Are you hurting?" she asked curiously, unable to remove her fascinated gaze from his penis as it grew longer and harder under her caressing hand. She joined her right hand to the left and drew them both firmly down from the root to the tip and back again. "You feel so amazing! So soft on the outside, and rock hard inside," she whispered, leaning down to kiss the tip.

He groaned louder than ever; his hand thrust into her hair as he held her head. It was an effort not to push himself into her wandering mouth. But he didn't want to shock her. Nor hurt her for that matter. "Shrey?"

"Mmm?" She lifted her gaze to his tortured face, licking the bead of moisture which had formed on the tip of his shaft.

"Let go, sweetheart," he said, his body shuddering with need.

Taking her mouth off him, she asked, "You don't like it?"

"Where did you learn to do that?" he asked curiously.

She shrugged once slender shoulder, unaware of her jiggling breast. "I read a lot, you know."

"Oh!" He lifted a mocking eyebrow, his eyes half shut as he continued to thrust himself into her clever hands as she pumped him.

"Are you being sarcastic?" she asked, giving him a mocking glance, by now too confident about his attraction for her.

"Never," he declared, removing her hands firmly before pushing her down on the bed and lying between her legs. Kissing her mouth deeply, he said, "I want to dive inside you."

"What's stopping you?" she asked, her hands caressing his wide shoulders.

Chirag cursed when he suddenly realised he had been about to enter her without wearing a condom. Reaching over towards the table at the side of his bed, he tore open a packet before sheathing himself. "This is bound to hurt, sweetheart," he said apologetically. "I'll try to be as gentle as possible."

Her gaze turned wary as she looked at the way he was thrusting his chin in a determined fashion. *How bad was it going to be?* But she forgot her own name when he leaned down to make love to her breasts, suckling her so deeply she was sure she was going to climax once again, without him having to enter her body.

Chirag pushed a finger into her core and gave a satisfied grunt when it came away wet. Pulling her leg around his waist, he smiled when she lifted her other leg to lock her ankles at the small of his back. "Good girl," he said, his hands on her thighs as he parted her wider before placing the tip of his shaft against the entrance to her vagina. Taking a deep breath, he thrust into her in a single stroke, his heart breaking when he heard her scream of pain. His arms trembling with pressure as he pressed his hands on the bed at both her sides, he leaned down to kiss her lips. "I'm so sorry, sweetheart," he apologised sweetly, waiting for her to adjust to his invasion of her body.

Unlocking her legs, she moved them restlessly when she felt a strange urge within her as she twisted and turned to adapt her body to him.

He couldn't wait any longer as Chirag pulled out of her to push right within. This time, there was no barrier to stop him.

Shreya moaned loudly when she felt him enter her a second time. But this time, it was so different from the first, making her melt. She lifted her lower body, and tried to match his rhythmic thrusts and soon they were pounding into each other as they reached over to the climax which seemed so close, but so out of reach. She clawed at his back in excitement, her throat turning raw with her shrieks as the pleasure built up within her, lifting her towards the skies. Then, one long scream and she fell over the edge, tumbling into an abyss, her body feeling weightless. She was sure she would have fallen off the surface of the earth if Chirag had not been there to catch her back.

A moment later, he flopped down on her slender body with a long and loud groan, like a limp rag, the mind numbing orgasm having ripped him to shreds. He tried to move, but found himself unable to, his breaths coming in gasps, and his body having become as weak as a new born kitten's.

Shreya wrapped her arms around him, holding him close as she took long and deep breaths, hoping to stabilise her heartbeat in the next hundred or so years.

"Don't wanna hurt you," he mumbled, his face buried against her breasts, his eyes shut tightly. He couldn't have moved a single muscle, not even to save his life.

"You aren't," she responded briefly, stroking his back gently. "Go to sleep."

And he did just that. Shreya followed him, barely seconds later, a smile on her lips.

13

"**S**hreya." Ambika sat down next to her daughter, affectionately stroking her slender back.

"Mom." Shreya kept her phone aside to lean her head on her mother's shoulder.

"Listen, I know we agreed not to…"

Shreya straightened up to sit away from her mother, lifting an eyebrow, too aware of how the gesture bothered Ambika.

"Don't give me that look, girl, and listen to me," ordered Ambika, trying to appear stern. The trouble was that Ambika was a loving and lenient mother, even if she kept on coming up with prospective bridegrooms for her reluctant child.

After Kunal Choksi, three men had been rejected on the basis of their photographs, Shreya taking her father Sunil's support to refuse the alliances. And thank God, she hadn't needed to meet any of them in person.

"I am, Mom, I am."

"There is this alliance." She lifted a hand when Shreya would have protested. "Listen to me fully. His name is Chirag Bhatia and he has his own advertising…" Ambika paused when she saw Shreya get up from the sofa. "Aren't you going to listen to me fully?"

Shreya turned away, unable to believe her ears. *Has Chirag, my Chirag, decided to get married?* Hadn't he mentioned only the earlier evening he had no such plans, for at least four or five years? Oh yes, Shreya and Chirag met regularly at his ground floor apartment, at least on ten evenings during the last two weeks after the first time they made love. They were having loads of fun, without a thought about the future.

Turning back to her mother in a flash, she asked, "Are you speaking about the same Chirag Bhatia who was at the Ahujas' party?" she asked.

Ambika frowned, thinking. "Was he? I don't remember meeting him or his parents. Rekha is a common friend…" She stopped speaking when she noticed Shreya was saying something.

"Isn't she always?" muttered Shreya, pouting her lips before blowing air upwards to ease her irritation.

"Did you say something?" Ambika asked, not hearing Shreya's whispered words. When her daughter shook her head, she continued, "Let me ask Rekha to send me a photo, and I'll share it with you."

Shreya threw her hands up in the air. "Mom, listen. For the last time, I don't want to get married, not in the near future."

"But why?" squealed Ambika, staring at her daughter, aghast. No one listening to the mother-daughter duo would come to know the two of them had had the same argument multiple times.

"Mom! Why should I get married now? Girls my age don't these days. For that matter, even you got married at twenty-six. I…"

"I'm going to kill your father for telling you that," swore Ambika. "But listen, Shreya. My case was different.

My parents tried to set up my marriage, so many times, from the day I turned nineteen. Only, nothing worked out; at least, not before I met your father."

Crossing her arms over her chest, Shreya impatiently tapped her foot on the floor, waiting for her mother to finish what she had to say. She preferred to believe Chirag, and was sure he would have never agreed to a bride hunt. *Rekha Aunty is an idiot,* fumed Shreya.

"So, listen. Rekha is organising a meeting with the Bhatias. They have two older daughters who are already married. There is only one son, it seems."

"No."

"Who is a super successful businessman… wait, what do you mean by no?" Ambika gave her daughter a frustrated glance.

"Mom, listen. If you don't stop this, right now, I'm going to catch the next flight out of Delhi and return to Durban, okay? I cannot put up with this torture any longer," said Shreya in a firm voice.

"You are being rude," wailed Ambika, her eyes filming over with tears.

Aware of her mother's dramatic leanings, Shreya refused to fall for the crocodile tears. "I don't want to be. But you are forcing my hand."

"But what will I tell Rekha? She has been working so hard, lining up suitable grooms. All her hard work will simply go to waste," Ambika wailed some more. The tears had stopped abruptly though, when she realised they didn't move her daughhter, not by an iota.

"Too bad. But then, it's her business to bring couples together. I am sure she understands all about winning some, and losing some," Shreya said firmly, pinning her mother's gaze with her own.

"I never expected this of you, Shreya."

"Well, now you are clear." She had the last word before leaving the hall and going to her bedroom. The first thing Shreya did was to call Chirag, not too bothered it was the middle of a work day.

"Hey, sweetheart!" Chirag couldn't stop the smile which lit up his face as he turned his chair to face the floor-length window in his office, gazing out at the landscape. Last night had been too damn fantastic, and he couldn't wait to see her again; make love to her sexy body.

"Are you aware that your name is topping the list for prospective bridegrooms?" she directly came to the point.

"What?" Chirag removed the phone from his ear to stare down at it for a couple of seconds before placing it against his ear once again. "Who told you that?"

"I believe Rekha Aunty has your name on the list. My mother just now tried to convince me to go meet you and your family."

He gave a startled laugh. "What did you tell her?"

"You find it funny?" she asked, trying to whip up her anger. But she realised she was too enamoured with him to feel annoyed. A gurgle escaped her lips before she began to laugh in earnest as well.

"What did you tell your mother?" he asked, once she finished laughing, curious to know her reaction.

"That she had better stop with this nonsense. Or I'd take the next flight back to Durban."

"Good for you. Though I'm hoping you're going to stay right here in Delhi until the end of your planned two months." There were still four weeks to go.

"Oh yes, I do." She had never expected it would be so awesome, having a love affair. But it truly was. So freeing too! Chirag was a considerate lover, always caring for her needs. And even better was the fact that he gave her the confidence to explore her own sexuality. No, she wasn't going to think about the other truth—that she was speedily and surely falling in love with him. "But tell me something, are your parents looking for a bride for you?"

"They had better not. And no, I don't think so. It's probably Rekha Aunty's idea. I'm sure I'll get to know all about it this evening."

"Are you planning to go to your bungalow?" she asked, unable to hide the disappointment in her voice.

"Yep. Mom called in the morning today and I'd better go to see them. Hey, do you want to go meet Jack and Jill?" he asked. He could always take her back to his apartment after dinner.

"I think not. If my mother knows your name, I'm sure your mother will be aware..."

"Ouch! And my mother will recognise your name too."

Shreya sighed. "I hope they don't begin to put two and two together..."

"I'm sorry, sweetheart. I..."

"But why are you sorry? It's not your fault."

"Hmm, you're right."

"I have a sneaky feeling your mother must have called you for this very reason..."

Chirag had arrived at the same conclusion by now. "I have the same sneaky feeling too," he said, a light of battle entering his eyes.

"Well, wish you luck," she said, unable to stop the giggle which escaped her throat.

"For what?" he growled, frowning.

"Facing your parents; telling them you don't want to meet any prospective bride... meaning me..." She giggled some more, unable to complete her sentence.

"I have a good mind to agree to this meeting and see where it takes us," he said, wishing he was in the same room as her. He so wanted to tickle her ribs until her giggles made her breathless.

"You wouldn't!"

"You think so?" he asked lazily, leaning back on his chair, enjoying the panic in her voice.

"Chirag!"

"What?"

"You don't want to take the *saat phere*, not at twenty-eight!" There was a note of desperation in Shreya's voice.

"Maybe I've changed my mind," he teased, biting his lip to stop himself from laughing.

"I think I'll go," she told him in a weak voice, wondering if her lover of last night had gone mad. No, the prospect of marriage, even with Chirag, didn't excite her. He was based in Delhi, running his super successful ad agency, while she had a rocking career in Durban, building towards running her own yoga studio in the not-too-far future. There was no way the ends could meet. Right now, she was looking forward to having a long-distance relationship with him, after she went back to Durban. And not at all ready for a life-long commitment.

"Wait, Shreya, don't go. You know I was only teasing you. Of course I don't want to get married, not for a long while."

"What are you going to do?" she asked. "Do you plan to tell your parents?"

"They already know my intentions. Let me go and find out what has changed."

"Okay. We'll not be able to meet tonight, then," she said, abject disappointment in her voice.

He made a sound of frustration. "True. But tomorrow, I promise."

"Okay." She blew him a kiss before signing off, visualising his adorable face.

"Mom!" Chirag stepped into his bungalow and hugged his mother.

"You are becoming a stranger, Chirag," grumbled Chandrika, hugging her tall and strapping son with enthusiasm.

"Are you missing me?" he asked her teasingly.

"Jack and Jill miss you, more than I do," she said, a tad sarcastic.

He gave her a cheeky grin, not really surprised when he felt the two cats climbing over his legs, as they dug their sharp nails into his corduroy pants. "You little guys," he greeted them, removing the cats one by one from where they were clinging to his pants and tucking them into his elbows. Cuddling them, he went to sit on the sofa.

"Will you have coffee?" she asked, as it was barely six. In fact, she was surprised he had come home so early. Chirag rarely left his place of work before eight in the evening.

He didn't plan to tell his mother that he worked lesser hours these days. And also, he was still hoping he could have an early dinner and make time to meet Shreya. "Yes, Mom. Where's Dad?"

"Must be on his way home," she said, going to the kitchen to ask Ramu *kaka* to bring coffee and some light snacks.

Once the cook left the coffee tray along with two bowls brimming with homemade *bhujia* and *masala puri*, Chandrika directly came to the point. She was glad Chirag was here before her husband was home; she didn't want father and son to clash regarding the alliance which had unexpectedly come up for her son. Pouring the pre-mixed coffee into two mugs, she offered him one before clearing her throat. "Listen, Chirag. I know what you told me, but..."

"Eh?" Chirag lifted an eyebrow at his mother, even as he fed bits of the fried snacks to his pets, both Jack and Jill gobbling them up before asking for more. "What did I tell you?" he asked. It looked like he and Shreya had guessed correctly.

"*Wohi!* That you want to get married only after four years or so..."

"What's different now?" he asked.

Chandrika cleared her throat once again. It wasn't as if she was afraid of her son. Chirag was a good son and usually had an even temperament. But he also had a temper which blew up at times. And he had made it clear the subject of his marriage was taboo, for at least the next few years. But what could she do? Rekha was so persuasive.

"Listen, that girl you brought home for dinner some weeks ago, Shreya... do you know her parents are looking out for an alliance for her?" He had said she was a friend. What in case her son wanted this Shreya to be more than a friend?

"Yes, of course. Rekha Aunty had fixed a meeting with Nishaan and his parents for the same reason."

"Oh! I didn't know that."

Of course, his mother didn't know that. "It was at Nishaan's house that I met Shreya." Chirag preferred to stick to the truth as much as possible; though he didn't have any qualms about omitting stuff from his parents.

"Do you like her?" asked Chandrika eagerly.

"Of course I like her, Mom. She's my friend." Well, he couldn't be more casual than that, could he?

Chandrika valiantly smiled despite the fact that the corners of her mouth were curving southwards. "Well, it's like this. Rekha asked me if you might be interested in meeting Shreya formally?" She didn't have the guts to continue further as she lifted her gaze to her son.

"Why would I want to do that?" he asked, giving his mother a sharp glance. He ignored the way his heart was thumping so loudly in his rib cage. Any talk of Shreya made his blood soar, it seemed.

"I have an idea, Chirag." Chandrika went off at a tangent when she noticed the grim expression on her son's face.

"Hmm."

"You obviously like Shreya. And I'm sure she likes you too." She checked his face for any signs of a rising temper before continuing, "I was thinking, why not the two of you get engaged? Maybe you can get married a couple of years from now." She gave him a broad smile before she settled back on the sofa, relieved to have gotten the matter off her chest.

"Why would we want to get engaged?" Chirag's voice was a murmur. It was with great difficulty he wasn't snarling by now. He loved his mother, and didn't want to hurt her unnecessarily.

"As I said, it was an idea." She looked at him expectantly.

He went on his knees before her, taking her hands in his before speaking. Believing it was a new game, the two cats climbed on his calves and settled down comfortably to lick themselves. "Not a good one, Mom. I'm sorry to disappoint you. But I don't want to marry Shreya, or anyone else. Please try to understand me, Mom."

Tch! Chandrika's smile disappeared completely as she looked down at her son. She couldn't really understand why he didn't want to get married, and asked him outright. "What's your problem with getting married?"

"Mom… you know I'm still building my business and I work all kinds of strange hours. Do you want my wife to feel neglected?" he asked reasonably.

"How do you expect it to be different four years down the line?" she asked, glaring at him.

He gave her a pacifying grin. "I have a long-term plan, you see. My income will increase exponentially over the next few years, and I will be able to employ senior staff who can take part of my load."

"This is exactly why your father was keen for you to get a job," she grumbled.

He laughed outright. "That would be worse, Mom. I would have turned into a corporate slave, not even finding time for myself, let alone a wife."

Freeing her hands from his, she got up abruptly, unable to swallow her disappointment. She liked Shreya Udhas, a lot. And had been dreaming of having the young lady for son's wife from the moment Rekha made the suggestion. "You do what you want," she told him, walking away to the kitchen.

Chirag pushed the cats off his legs before getting up to follow his mother. Reaching her in two strides, he hugged her and kissed the top of her head. "Don't be angry, Mom. I love you."

She slapped him on his shoulder, smiling through her tears. "I know. That's why I put up with you."

"You just put up with me, do you?" he asked, giving her a mischievous grin.

She slapped him once again. "Don't be silly. You know I love you, Chirag."

"Thanks, Mom."

"I can't believe you are leaving tomorrow." Chirag held Shreya close to his chest as they lay on his bed, satiated for the moment after two rounds of energetic sex. It had been more than a month since they had become lovers and the time had flown on wings. It was the longest affair he had ever had.

"Mmm." She couldn't utter another syllable to save her life as Shreya lay in the warm cocoon of her lover's arms, her throat choked with emotion. She was head over heels in love with Chirag and never wanted to part with him, ever. Not that it meant she wanted to be married. Just like Chirag, she liked her single state and was not ready for commitment either. But that still hadn't stopped her from losing her heart to him.

These past few weeks had been mind-blowing; the secret meetings and the heated lovemaking, she had loved them all. And she couldn't imagine how she was going to live without seeing him at least a few times in a week. The distance between Delhi and Durban was so much, they couldn't meet for more than probably once in a year. But will Chirag even remember her face a few months from now, once she was out of his sight? She wasn't so sure. And she couldn't really blame him.

He had never promised her anything more than a hot, steamy affair. Even he seemed to be surprised by the fact that it had lasted this long.

Chirag looked down at the top of her head, his heart giving an unfamiliar lurch when he realised she was shaking in his arms. If he knew Shreya well, it was with emotion, though she would never trouble him with it. She had accepted his terms of non-commitment, and seemed happy spending time with him, both in and out of bed. But the ever-talkative Shreya going silent obviously meant something deep. With a long drawn out sigh shuddering from the depth of his being, he gently ran his hand down her slender back, stroking it repeatedly, doing his best to soothe her angst.

What Chirag hadn't expected was the feeling of emptiness invading him. He was going to miss her, terribly. He, Chirag, who didn't know the meaning of missing people. And it hit him hard, now that she was leaving tomorrow, that he might not see her again, not in many months. After all, this trip she had made to Delhi, was the first in a dozen years. It might take her another dozen to return to the Indian capital. Okay, maybe he could visit her in Durban. But how often could he do that?

"Shrey, do you like to travel?" he asked, in a follow up to his meandering thoughts.

She lifted her ragged face to his, a question in her eyes. "I like to travel, though I haven't been around much. Only to Johannesburg and now to Delhi." This time round, her mother had taken her siblings on a trip to Jodhpur, Udaipur and Jaipur for ten days. Even Tina had gone along with them. But Shreya had refused in the pretext of keeping her father company, as Sunil was fully tied up with his work. This was mainly because she hadn't been keen to be away from Chirag.

"Do you think we can plan trips to places around the world? Let's fix up to meet in Paris, maybe? In about three months? Can you get away for a week?" He sat up against the bedhead to pull her on his lap, liking his own idea.

Shreya's heart pumped heavily, a small smile breaking out on her sad face. So! He didn't want to break off permanently. At least, not for now. "I think I can manage that." She reached up to kiss his rough cheek. "And I would love to go to Paris with you."

"Perfect, I'll set the ball rolling as soon as possible. I have my calendar planned for the next six months. I…"

"Oh! Will you be able to take a break in March then?"

"I'm sure I can manage. What's the use of having a large staff if they cannot help me run the company?" he asked rhetorically.

"Oh, Chirag! I love this idea of yours. Thank you."

"Why are you thanking me?" he growled, "Can't you see I'm being totally selfish here?" He wasn't ready to admit to more than that. He couldn't imagine his life without Shreya, at least not in the immediate future. And he refused to think beyond the next few months. Holding her face in both his hands, he leaned down to kiss her hungrily, meticulously exploring her delicious mouth with his tongue.

Shreya leaned into his kiss with a deep sigh, grabbing him with both her hands on his wide shoulders. Her upper body came flush against his hard chest, her soft breasts crushed against his steely muscles, rejoicing in the contact.

Without breaking the kiss, Chirag slid down the bed, dragging her along with him before rolling her on to her back and settling on top of her. Finally letting go of her mouth, he kissed his way down her neck and shoulders and reached down to worship her breasts. By now, he was familiar with all her erogenous zones as he nibbled on her pulse points before suckling her breasts greedily in turn.

She dug her nails into his shoulders, her legs wrapped around his lean waist, gasping his name every time he touched a sensitive spot on her body. She let her head fall back on the pillows when a deep sigh left her as he worshipped her breasts. She clutched his head, her fingers holding tightly to his silky hair as she thrust her breasts, in turn, closer to his marauding lips, revelling in his rough caresses. His name was a chant on her lips as she called out to him in the throes of passion.

Chirag moved further down her body, not forgetting to give his attention to her ticklish ribs before exploring her navel with the tip of his tongue.

Before she could catch her breath, she lost it again when he rubbed his face against her vagina, making her gasp at the incredible sensation. *This is something I will never get used to,* thought Shreya, Chirag using his mouth to bring her to a climax. It had been the first time last week, when he had made love to her with that clever tongue of his and she had been transported to another realm. She had refused to say anything when he asked her about it, feeling too shy and awkward about the experience. While she didn't want to speak about it, she had secretly craved for him to make love to her, the same way, once again.

And here he was, granting her, her most secret desire, even before she could ask. "Chiraaaag…" She moaned when she felt him press his lips to her vagina.

He held her thighs down with his large hands as he kneeled between her legs to explore her feminine core. He lifted his gaze to hers when he heard her moan of delight, his name a sigh on her lips. "I take it that you don't dislike it?" he asked her lazily, an arrogant smile on his face, even as a dark eyebrow went up in gentle query.

"No, no, no, no," she said, shaking her head vigorously, a tad worried he might stop.

"Eh? Does that mean you don't want me to continue?" He knew only too well she had enjoyed it the first time; and also loved it now when he kissed her. But he wanted her to confirm it in so many words.

"What?" She sat up on hearing his words, her breasts bouncing in agitation. "Don't you dare stop," she commanded, the Aquarius coming to wild life.

He threw back his head to laugh before reaching forward to push her back on the bed. "I don't plan to," he promised, before going down on her again.

How many nerves do I have there? Shreya choked when she felt his tongue exploring each and every one of those with careful precision, her eyes rolling back in her head even as she forgot to breathe. It was as if there were only two things in the world: her vagina and his tongue. Everything else had disappeared. The tension built up, slowly, hotly, steadily, lustily. And Shreya felt herself being lifted on a cresting wave, up, up, up. Her body had gone weightless! So light that she felt as if she was floating among wispy clouds. *Or have I simply died and gone to heaven?* But if that were the case, what was this urge pushing from deep within her, trying to break barriers?

She heard a scream, long and loud, her body stretched taut as a bow, her hands clutching the comforter for purchase as she tumbled through the clouds, now slow, now fast, and then, a deep thud; she had fallen off the edge of the universe, her throat raw, her heart pounding, while her breath seemed to be lost for ever.

Chirag moved up to lie next to her, pulling the comforter around both of them as he pulled her back to his front, spoon fashion, before holding her close.

Shreya lay there in his arms, gaining her breath after what seemed to be a long time, her heavy eyelids shutting over her drenched eyes before sleep swathed her in its warmth.

"So, what's the plan?" Aadhira asked her sister in a whisper as they waited for their flight to be called.

"What plan?" Shreya frowned at her sister. She had just then finished speaking to Chirag and her heart was heavy.

"You and Chirag, of course. Duh!" Aadhira rolled her eyes to the ceiling and back before fixing it on Shreya's pinched face. She felt her sister's pain and had been holding her hand in silent support throughout the ride to the airport, the check in and now during the wait to board the flight.

"Tch! Don't really know." Shreya didn't want to speak about their Paris trip, not at all confident they could pull it off. First of all, Chirag was too damn busy with his work, also the reason why he didn't want to get married for the next few years, as he had no time for a fiancée or a wife. As for Shreya, it wasn't as if she had never been on trips with her friends from school and college. Her parents had always encouraged her to be independent. But she was simply scared of raising her hopes too high. What in case he forgot all about it? After all, wasn't there a saying—out of sight, out of mind?

"Didn't you mention Paris?" Aadhira prodded.

"Aadhi, I know you love me and all. But can we talk about something else? Or we can remain silent too." Shreya didn't really care she was being rude, that too, to her younger sister who was only being a loving support. But how she wished she could stop thinking about Chirag! The best solution to this was to throw herself into her work. Maybe she would offer to do two shifts, instead of one. Yes, that's what she planned to do, once she got back to Durban.

"Okay, if that's what you want. I think I'm going to check out the shops." Aadhira got up from her chair. "Wanna come?"

"You go. I'll..."

"I'll let you wallow in your self-pity," said Aadhira, walking backwards.

Shreya showed her sister the middle finger before burying her face in the book she was carrying, totally unaware she was holding it upside down.

It was half an hour later when Aadhira walked back with two ice-cream cones, handing the butterscotch flavour—Shreya's favourite—to her sister in a peace offering. What she hadn't expected was for Shreya to tear up when she accepted the ice-cream. After all, how was Aadhira to know it was a tub of butterscotch ice-cream the lovers had shared on the last night they had spent together?

Shreya sniffed loudly before squaring her shoulders, wiping her eyes with a tissue. Okay, she loved a man who was not in love with her. Okay, she might never set eyes on him again. Or maybe they might meet on and off over the next… couple of years? Maybe more; maybe less. What was there to cry about? She was young, she was healthy, she was energetic. She had a rocking career she was passionate about; which also helped her stay healthy and fit. Shreya decided to count her blessings and simply lead a happy life.

That set the tone for the next few months as Shreya threw herself into her work and partied long and hard during the weekends, glad to be with familiar faces, who might never think of spiking her dessert with drugs.

Yes, I am happy, because I choose to be!

15

All of Shreya's worry and fear were completely unnecessary. Not a day went by without Chirag going on a video call with his long-distance girlfriend. While Shreya helped keep him grounded—the yoga sessions with her went a long way in doing that too—she also made him crave her all the more. What he needed was a space capsule which could take him to her at the speed of thought. But then, if wishes were horses, wouldn't beggars ride too?

It was an effort to keep a firm lid on his effervescent temper, and Chirag seemed to lose it at the drop of a hat. But what actually woke him up to the truth was when he received an email of resignation from his long-standing executive assistant, Vikrant Bakshi. Vikrant had been with Chirag right from the time the latter set up his advertising agency, and was not only a diligent employee, but was someone whom Chirag had come to trust enough to run the company smoothly even during the CEO's absence. Chirag had a plan to make Vikrant Bakshi his company's Vice President in the not-too-distant future.

He was shocked out of his wits when Vikrant sent him a crisp and polite email before nine in the morning:

Dear Chirag,

It has been a wonderful and fruitful five years, working as your executive assistant at Chibha. But the time has come for me to move on. Kindly treat this mail as my notice of resignation, beginning today. I will remain with the company for the full term of two months' notice period, and train the person you select to take my responsibilities from here on.

I thank you for all your support. I need to mention here that I have learnt a lot from you and have gained nothing but great experiences here.

Warm regards,
Yours faithfully,
Vikrant Bakshi

Chirag called Vikrant on his cell. "Do you have a minute, buddy?"

"Of course, Chirag."

"Come over to my office." Chirag disconnected the phone, not bothering to wait for Vikrant's response. He called the kitchen and asked for coffee and cookies while he waited for his executive assistant. He lifted a hand to wave Vikrant in when he knocked on the cabin door. "Have a seat," invited Chirag, studying Vikrant's face, a tad disturbed when the younger man refused to meet his gaze.

"Thanks," muttered Vikrant, plopping into the chair across his boss's desk. He steepled his hands, as if in penance as he rested his elbows on the table, waiting for Chirag to speak.

Chirag lifted his hand once again when the canteen help brought the tray he had requested for. Pointing to a spot between the two of them, Chirag told the boy to leave the tray in the middle of the table. He cleared his throat loudly once the server left. "Okay, Vikrant, now tell me. What's the issue? Have you got another offer? Maybe a better one?" he asked, absolutely confident he was paying his assistant the best possible salary in the present-day job market. Lifting the plate of cookies, he offered it to Vikrant.

"Thanks," muttered Vikrant once again, taking a cookie and biting into it. He still refused to look at Chirag's face.

Chirag poured the coffee from the flask, into the two mugs and pushed the tray towards the other man, watching Vikrant keenly as he picked up a mug. He didn't miss the tremor in Vikrant's hand. "Why do you want to leave?"

Vikrant lifted his pained gaze to his boss. It was as if he was saying, 'need you ask?' without uttering a word.

A deep sigh shuddered through Chirag. "It has been difficult to work with me this last month." It was no question, but a declaration.

Vikrant lifted one shoulder in a shrug. Boss and employee had always shared an honest relationship. And Vikrant had never had any qualms about pointing out a mistake whenever Chirag committed any. Which was all the more reason why Chirag valued him. He had grown too fast, too big, in the last few years that there were barely one or two people who had the guts to stand up to him.

"Damn it, Vik! Say something *yaar*." Chirag slapped the table with the palm of his hand, making a sound like a gunshot.

Vikrant took a moment to place his half-drunk mug of coffee on the tray before getting up to stand, drawing himself up to his full height of six feet two inches. Looking down his hawk-like nose at Chirag, he said, "This is exactly why I want to quit, damn you. You aren't the man I met half a dozen years ago. You are a wreck, Chirag. Your evil temper has got the better of you. The man I knew, the one from whom I learnt everything about the ad business I know today, seems to have changed, and definitely not for the better. I cannot work under this kind of pressure, not knowing when you will take off like a rocket without a moment's notice. It's my job to help you run your business, not to play your mother. And no, I don't have another job to go to. And I don't think I'll get a job which I will enjoy as much as I used to like this one." Vikrant spoke in a quiet, but firm voice, his words sharp, punching Chirag like bullets.

"*Ho gaya?*" asked Chirag, his voice calm, like the one which comes before a storm.

"I think so."

"Be sure! And that's an order." Chirag's voice rose in pitch.

"I'm done. And I am leaving, NOW." Vikrant turned to step towards the cabin door.

"Sit down, you bastard. And face me like a man." Chirag spat the words, his chest heaving with the control he placed over his quaking temper.

"Face you like a man?" Vikrant snarled as he turned around with a jerk, placing his hands on the table as he leaned down to glare into Chirag's face. "If I had done that already, I would have put your patrician nose out of joint, literally. And broken your handsome jaw, so you wouldn't be able to speak for at least a week."

Chirag's eyes went wide in shock. He would have never believed Vikrant had such a violent temper if someone had told him. But even before Chirag's own temper could blow out of control, his ever-present humour—the mark of a true Sagittarius—came to his rescue as he threw back his head and laughed uproariously. Getting up from his chair, he walked around the desk to stand next to Vikrant, and patted him on his shoulder. "I'm sorry, *yaar*. Forgive me?"

Vikrant crossed his arms over his massive chest as he continued to glare at his boss, impatiently tapping his foot on the wooden floor. Lifting an eyebrow in query, he asked sarcastically, "For what?"

"For being such a pain in the ass…"

"You said it," declared Vikrant, his deep brown eyes twinkling with a smile. "I'm glad you finally noticed."

Chirag grimaced. "How could I not? But tell me something. Is it just you? Or more of the office is ready to walk out on me as well?"

"You do realise I've been standing like a solid pillar between you and the others, protecting the rest of the office staff, don't you?"

His grimace changing into a scowl, Chirag said, "It's going to be chaos if you leave…"

Vikrant didn't gloat, but said in a matter-of-fact voice, "That's true."

"Do you want me to beg?"

"Why don't you marry her and put all of us out of this misery?" asked Vikrant, his head tilted back as he gazed boldly at his boss. The words were those of a man who was confident of his own worth.

Chirag shook his head firmly. "That's not a solution."

Vikrant sighed exaggeratedly. "You aren't giving me a choice here…"

"Wait! Don't be in a hurry. I'll…"

"Have you considered anger management classes?" asked Vikrant, laughing by now. "No, I mean seriously."

A glimmer of a smile appeared on Chirag's face. "You do drive a point home, buddy. I receive your message, loud and clear. So, what can I offer you to keep you here? A ten per cent increase in your pay packet? Maybe a…"

Vikrant didn't let him finish what he was saying, shaking his head from side to side. "I don't need a pay raise. All I ask for is a peaceful work environment. Think you can manage that?"

Chirag grimaced. "I can try…"

"Not good enough." Vikrant was firm in his rebuttal.

"Was it so bad?" asked Chirag, surprised on hearing Vikrant's words.

"Worse. I will accept nothing less than a promise from you. And one more thing, the next time you roar like a lion, I quit, without a moment's notice."

Chirag burst out laughing. He took Vikrant's hand in his and shook it vigorously. "I promise. And welcome back on board, my friend. I can't manage my agency without you."

"Thank you, Chirag." Vikrant gave him a relieved smile.

Shreya didn't stop laughing for a long time that evening when Chirag told her about the incident during their daily call.

"Go on, laugh all you want," growled Chirag, a smile in his black eyes as he watched her adorably expressive face, "only I can't see what's funny about this situation."

"Can't you? My darling Chirag, listen. We both are keen to build our respective careers in two different hemispheres. But we also want to spend time together whenever possible. I think we can manage to do that for a few days, once every quarter. I think we should thank our lucky stars we can afford to holiday every few months. What more do you want? Under the circumstances, I mean?" While Shreya tried to beat him with her logic, she herself yearned to be near him, within touching distance. But that was like asking for the moon.

Chirag glared at her, not saying anything. She was right, of course. But that still didn't stop him from feeling so damn frustrated. He missed her, like one would miss an arm or a leg. "I want you in my arms," he said, his words coming out in a tortured growl.

"I know, baby, I know. I want to be in your arms too."

"That does it. I'm taking a flight to Durban tomorrow. We can spend the weekend together. I…"

Shreya's heart almost burst out of her chest when she heard his words. "Are you sure?"

"Yes."

"Will you come to my house?" she asked, a wary expression on her face. Her parents were modern, especially now that they were back home in Durban. But even they wouldn't take kindly to her inviting her lover home.

He shook his head. "I don't think that will work. Er… won't you join me at my hotel? Wherever I plan to stay?"

Shreya thought about it for a few moments, not giving her reply.

"Shrey?"

This hurried and hashed up trip was only going to leave him more frustrated. And it was going to be so expensive too. While they were all rolling in money, it still didn't mean they should squander it. "How about we plan it better? I can take a whole week off in another month, as I work on all seven days. I…"

Chirag stared at her, aghast. "Oh, sweetheart! You've been working all days of the week? What are your bosses? Slave drivers?"

Shreya shook her head. "Of course not. I asked for this only because I wanted to take a break every few months, so that we could meet. Isn't that what we planned?" she asked.

He always knew she was intelligent. Oh yes, his Shreya was extremely smart; and better planned then even he was. "True."

"Why don't we stick to the plan? Now, shall we do yoga?" she asked.

"I don't want to do yoga!"

"Chirag, don't be a child."

"I'm not."

"You are too. Losing your cool isn't going to help either of us."

"I hate your logic," he grumbled.

"Would you rather I lost my temper too?" she asked, a glint in her brown gaze.

"Okay, you win." He put up both his hands in surrender. "Now tell me what to do."

Shreya blew him a kiss before teaching him the various postures of the *Surya Namaskar*.

It was Paris in March; and Singapore in June. Later, they went on a trip to Mauritius in October. The third week of December found them in Sydney, to celebrate Chirag's birthday on the nineteenth.

Shreya arrived on the fifteenth, reaching The Grace Hotel just before lunch local time. She checked into the Signature Premium Corner King Room which Chirag had already booked in their names. After a quick and refreshing shower, she went looking for lunch, as there were still three more hours to go before Chirag arrived.

She went to the pub—P.J. O'brien's Irish Pub—which was open throughout the day and ran her gaze through the menu, scrunching her nose as she searched long and hard for vegetarian options. Finally, she chose the *Alfredo Primavera Linguini*—a crunchy vegetable dish tossed in creamy Alfredo sauce, including cauliflower, broccoli, mushrooms, capsicum, and green beans. She ordered a pint of chilled light beer to drink along with her lunch. Sitting back to study her surroundings, Shreya's eyes lit up when she noticed the wooden flooring and staircase which led to the upper level. At one corner was the bar, the wood and glass shelves displaying the various brands of alcohol they served. A round clock held centre of place at the top of the bar with a guitar displayed in a glass case right below. The place had but a few customers at four in the evening, though people kept coming and going.

She smiled at the waiter who brought her beer, and thanked him sweetly.

"Your food should be here in fifteen minutes," he said, smiling right back at her in a friendly fashion.

"Thanks," said Shreya, sipping from her glass with a sigh of pleasure. It was simply perfect in the warm weather. She caught the gaze of a few other guests, smiling and nodding, though she wasn't keen on talking to anyone, preferring to be in her own world.

Her food arrived and she relished every bite of it, eating slowly, after ordering another pint of beer.

She decided to walk off her lunch as she went down to the street level, strolling leisurely down the length of the footpath, stopping at the many glass windows of the Grace Plaza to check out the branded goods on display from the multiple shops, the time passing quickly.

She smiled when her phone rang and she saw Chirag's darling face on the screen. "Hey! Have you reached?" she asked, her throat choking with excitement. Barely two months had gone since they last met, but it seemed like a couple of hundred years to her.

"I am in the hotel lobby."

"See you in five," she promised in a breathless voice as she rushed to the entrance to walk inside the coolness of the beautiful lobby with marble floor and brilliantly lit chandeliers. Seeing Chirag standing at the reception, she ran the rest of the way before throwing herself into his arms and lifting her face up for his kiss.

And he obliged her with alacrity, kissing her hungrily. It was a long while before they came up for air, not noticing one of the managers smiling at them—the same one who had been verifying Chirag Bhatia's identification.

"Miss me?" Chirag asked her in a hoarse voice.

"Horribly," she declared, reaching up to kiss him once again.

The manager, realising that he might have to interrupt the couple if he was to get his work done—after all, there was a small queue forming behind the two of them as more people were waiting to check into the hotel—cleared his throat loudly, smiling when the couple finally came apart. "I'm sorry to interrupt, Mr Bhatia."

"Not at all, mate." Chirag gave him a wink before signing the form and taking back his passport. "Thanks for your patience."

"We wish you a wonderful stay at The Grace Sydney, sir, madam."

Chirag gave him a nod before turning towards the lift, one arm wrapped around Shreya, while the other hand held his luggage.

"This way," said Shreya, turning him towards the bank of elevators. They took the lift to the tenth floor where their room was. She felt herself backed against the wall the moment they entered the room, Chirag pinning her with his body as he kissed her.

He pushed her thin top out of his way to explore her waist, his hands roaming up to cup her breasts, as he sighed with pleasure. "I missed you too, babe." He nuzzled her ear, nibbling on her lobe before trailing his lips down to kiss her rapidly beating pulse. "Mmm… you taste so damn good," he declared, stroking the tip of his tongue repeatedly over the pulse, smiling when he felt it leap under his caress.

She shoved the flaps of his jacket out of her way before unbuttoning his shirt with eager hands. When she couldn't slide either garment off his shoulders, all because he had his arms wrapped around her, she reached down to unbuckle his belt and jeans, pulling down the zipper eagerly. Her breath caught in her throat when her hand came against bare skin. She tilted her head back to look up at him with her amused gaze when he let go of her mouth. "Really?" she asked, lifting her eyebrows as she cupped her hand over his hardened shaft.

"What's a man to do?" he grumbled. "I've been like this even before I caught my flight back in Delhi. All because I was going to meet you soon."

"You poor baby," she laughed, though her eyes heated up, not just with pleasure but with the intensity of her desire. Going down on her knees, she dragged his jeans down his narrow hips, her nails scraping against the length of his thighs, shivering when she heard him groan. She leaned over to kiss his manhood, taking a quick lick from the root to the tip, laughing when she saw him spring forth eagerly. "Down!" she ordered, patting him mischievously, even as she lifted her dancing gaze to Chirag's.

"I don't think it's going to go down, not in the next forty-eight hours." His fingers splayed in her hair, Chirag held her head firmly as he stepped closer to her, moaning with pleasure when he felt her mouth close around his tip, her hands wrapped firmly around his length.

She licked him, she nibbled him, she pleasured him, enjoying the experience as much, if not more, than he was.

Chirag moved, or rather, his body moved of its own volition as he pushed into her and pulled back rhythmically, doing his best to be careful not to choke her. His legs trembled as he felt his shaft grow longer and tauter by the second. With extreme control, he pulled out of her mouth, placing his hands under her arms before lifting her up into his.

"Noooooo…" she protested. "I wanna more."

"Of course," he said, in a pacifying voice, though the fire raging in him was anything but soothing as he carried her over to the king-sized bed and placed her on it as if she was the most precious thing in the world. As he quickly divested himself of his shirt and jacket, he grinned as he watched her removing her short top and shorts. The smile disappeared from his face when his gaze fell on her bouncing breasts, with no bra to curtail them. Reaching with both hands, he cupped them before latching to one tip with his greedy mouth. "Mmm…" he hummed as he suckled her needily.

Shreya clutched his head in her hands as she pushed herself closer to his marauding mouth, unable to stop the moans which ensued from her throat.

He turned his head to make love with equal passion to her other breast, even as his hands roamed all over her body, fervently re-learning her shape.

Shreya, in turn, let go of his head to explore his smooth back, smiling when she ran her hands over the satiny skin stretched over such hard and well-packed muscles. Chirag used to swim and go for runs to keep fit. But nowadays, he also did yoga along with Shreya. And because of that his body was toned like never before. She dug her nails into his buttocks, moaning when he nipped the skin above her nipple in response.

"Ready?" he asked, spreading her legs wide to run a finger down the lips of her vagina.

"Always," she moaned, lifting her hips to accommodate him.

Giving her a roguish grin, he pulled her legs around his lean waist before entering her in a single stroke, grunting with satisfaction when he settled deep within her womb. Soon, they were pounding into each other as if there was no tomorrow, groaning and grunting as they reached out to the stars.

"Chiraaaag…" moaned Shreya when an explosive orgasm ripped through her.

It was a couple of minutes before Chirag followed her with a deep groan, falling over her, totally spent.

Wrapping her arms tightly around him, Shreya refused to let him go when he tried to move.

"I'm too heavy," he gasped.

"No," she disagreed, "you are perfect," and kissed the top of his head.

Not having slept a wink on the flight, despite travelling business class, Chirag went to sleep in Shreya's arms, not waking up for the next four hours.

"You shouldn't have let me sleep for so long," he protested, coming awake suddenly to look up at her. But it had been too damn cosy to sleep with his face buried against her breasts. He reached a lazy hand to tweak a tip, smiling when she gasped.

She ran her fingers through the thick locks of his hair, giving him a smile from her half-closed eyes. "You were out like the light."

"I'm sor…"

He didn't have a choice but to stop speaking when she placed a hand over his mouth, shaking her head. "I enjoyed having you in my control," she laughed, winking at him outrageously. "You must be hungry. Should I order some food?"

"I am," he said, laughing when his stomach growled on cue. "What time is it?" he asked.

"Almost ten."

"Let me have a quick shower and we'll go down to the restaurant. What say?"

"That would be lovely."

He slid up the bed to kiss her deeply. "Do you want to join me?" he asked, his hands roaming over her slender body, revelling in the texture of her silky skin.

She laughed, shaking her head. "That wouldn't really be a quick shower, will it? You go on."

"Are you sure?"

"Absolutely," she said, kissing his cheek. "Let's have dinner before returning right back to bed. Works?"

"Perfect," he said, getting out of the bed, not missing her admiring eyes as she ran them down the length of his body. "Irresistible, no?" he asked, the corners of his eyes crinkling with laughter.

"Temptation on legs," she agreed, blowing him a kiss.

"I'll see you soon."

Shreya quickly brushed her teeth and washed her face at the washbasin while he showered in the cubicle. Towelling herself dry, she went to the wardrobe to remove a short emerald green dress with a halter neck, made of silk. Removing a lacy pair of panties in the same shade of green, she set out to apply her make up first, using a light hand as she brushed green eye shadow over her eyelids before highlighting it with a dark brown eyeliner which made her brown eyes glow brilliantly. Wearing her panties, she pulled on the dress over her head just as

Chirag stepped out of the bathroom. She turned to him with a smile when he whistled softly.

"You look stunning," he declared, walking over to give her a kiss on her cheek. He didn't hug her as he was still damp from the shower. "That shade of green looks fab on you."

Soft colour running up her cheeks, she smiled at him through the mirror. "Thanks."

"Though I can't wait to take the dress off you," he concluded, giving her a devilish grin.

She laughed, happiness bubbling inside her now that she was with him, looking forward to the coming week. Blowing him a kiss, she stepped away from the dressing table, making space for him. "Would you like me to unpack for you?" she asked.

"Not fully," he said, removing the towel from his waist to dry himself vigorously. "Just a pair of pants, shirt and a jacket."

"Shall I choose?" she asked, opening his trolley case, which lay on the rack at a convenient height.

"Feel free," said Chirag, combing his hair.

She picked out a pair of cream cotton pants and a dark green full-sleeved t-shirt of soft cotton. "Is this okay?"

"Just what I'd have chosen," he said, giving her a cheeky grin.

"Very funny," she pouted at him. After all, he must know what was in his suitcase as he was the one who had packed it.

He got ready swiftly and wrapping his arm around her waist, drew her towards the elevator. "Still going vegetarian?" he asked, looking down at her. He had to hold himself back from kissing her luscious lips, but there were four other people in the elevator car, also going all the way down to the ground floor.

"You bet."

"What did you have for lunch?"

She told him. "Though that was one of the very few options at the pub."

"Would you like to check out some other restaurant? Or are you hungry?"

She shrugged. "I'd love to. How about you?"

"Now that my beast is tamed for the time being, I can handle my hunger for food. Let's go check out some new place," he whispered naughtily into her ear.

Shreya shivered when she felt the brush of his mouth against her ear, even as she laughed at his words. "Fine, let's do that."

"I know listening to the opera is a lifetime experience, but no way am I going to one," declared Chirag, his arm wrapped around Shreya's shoulders as they stood on the balcony attached to their hotel suite, which looked over the Sydney harbour. It was two days since they had arrived in the Australian city, and they had stepped out of the suite only for dinner so far.

Shreya laughed. "I agree. Why don't we simply do a tour of the Opera House? There's one which includes drinks and dinner." She reached up to kiss his cheek.

"Why not? Anything for you," he declared passionately before taking her mouth in a sizzling kiss. It was almost a year now, since they first made love, and he still could not get enough of her.

"Anything? There's this famous opera singer from…"

"No." He placed a hand over her mouth, gazing into her laughing eyes. "Anything but that."

"Mmm… now let me see…"

"Do you plan to torture me?" he asked, wrapping both his arms around her.

"Now why would I do that?" she asked, gurgling with laughter. "Want to go for a swim?"

"Let's go." He took her hand to go back into the bedroom. But it was another couple of hours before they left the suite as they got distracted while Shreya tried to change into her swimming costume.

After a few of hours of swimming, they returned to the room to have a shower together, before deciding to go down to the restaurant for a meal.

Shreya wore the dress he had bought for her locally, a fiery red sheath which left her shoulders bare, and had a slit down the length of one leg as it fell all the way to her ankles. "What do you think?" she asked, turning around slowly in a pirouette, pouting her red lips at him.

"I think it's best we leave before I begin undressing you," he said, heat in his gaze as he studied her sexy figure. "I want to eat you up, whole."

"I'll let you do that after we finish dinner. We do need the fuel, you know," she said, giving him a saucy wink as they stepped out of the suite. "And you look dashing in that tuxedo," she said, pressing her mouth to his once they stepped into the lift.

Colour rising on his handsome face, he returned her kiss avidly, only letting go of her mouth when the lift came to a stop on the ground floor where the restaurant was situated.

On the eve of Chirag's birthday, the two of them went out for dinner and dancing. After a few vodka shots, they were in high spirits, both literally and figuratively, as they swirled around energetically to the fast music and flashing lights of the disco.

Shreya kept track of the time on her watch, dragging him off the dance floor fifteen minutes before midnight. "Let's go back to the hotel," she said.

"But it's barely midnight," he protested. He loved to dance, especially with her, both fast and slow.

"Exactly," she told him, giving him a wink. They were within walking distance of The Grace Hotel and reached it in five minutes. Taking the elevator to the tenth floor, Chirag opened the door to their room, smiling widely when he saw the cake on the table, a single candle placed on it, with only the centre light on. "Oh!"

"Happy birthday, my darling Chirag," said Shreya, throwing her arms around his neck to kiss him on his mouth.

"Thank you." His voice was a gasp when they finally came up for air.

She left his arms to light the candle. "Barely a minute to go," she said in a breathless voice, "Come on, blow the candle," and she began to sing, "Happy birthday to you, happy birthday to you, happy birthday dear Chirag, happy birthday to you."

He blew the candle, smiling at her when she clicked pictures on her phone camera.

"I wanna kiss," he said.

"Don't you want to cut the cake?" she asked, her eyes shining with love and joy.

"Kiss first." He wrapped his arms across his chest, a determined thrust to his square chin.

Laughing, she stepped around the table to reach up to press her mouth to his, sighing softy when he kissed her right back with passion.

Finally, he let go of her mouth to take her hand in his before cutting the cake.

"Let me," she said, feeding him a piece, smiling when he in turn fed her some cake too.

"This is so yum," declared Chirag, licking her fingers, grinning when she licked his clean. "Where's my gift?" he asked, lifting an eyebrow.

"Gift? What gift?" she asked, pretending to be puzzled.

"My birthday gift, what else?" he asked, taking a threatening step towards her.

She giggled as she took a couple of steps back, shaking her head, before turning around and running to the other side of the room.

He caught her effortlessly before lifting her over his shoulder, his arms wrapped around the backs of her thighs as he carried her over to the bed.

"Chirag, put me down," she ordered, only it came out in a squeaky plea as she had gone breathless.

"In a moment." He let her slide down his front, holding her firmly within the circle of his arms, lifting an eyebrow in query. "I'm still waiting."

She shrugged. "Do you really want a gift?" she asked, giving him a mischievous smile.

"Of course, I do, yes."

"Well, in that case..." She kissed him on his cheek, her lips brushing against the fuzz which already covered his lean cheeks. Sliding her tongue into his mouth, she explored it leisurely, a deep humming sound emanating from her throat. It was a while before she let him go to walk over to the wardrobe where she had stored her suitcase. Opening the zip, she pulled out a small parcel wrapped in brightly coloured gift paper.

She turned around to find him standing close to her. "Here you go. Happy birthday."

"Thanks," he said, colour going up on his slashed cheeks. "What is it?" He shook it to check if he could take a guess.

Shreya shook her head at him. He was like a small child who had received his first birthday present.

But then, she wasn't to know this was the very first time Chirag was receiving a birthday gift from a woman who wasn't his relative. And he was damn excited about it. He opened the parcel slowly, folding the wrapper neatly before tucking it into his jacket pocket. In a three-inch square, it looked like a jeweller's box. Oh really! He lifted his gaze from the velvet box to look at Shreya, an eyebrow lifted in query.

She shook her head, continuing to smile, as she eagerly waited for him to open the box.

Chirag pressed the little button and the lid sprang open to reveal a silver bracelet, similar to a *kada* worn by men. "This looks so cool. What is it?" he asked, lifting it from the velvet bed to check it out. There were engravings of some exotic animals and birds, and it was finely crafted.

"It's a Berber bracelet, originating from Morocco; and it's handcrafted. Do you like it?"

"I love it," he declared, turning to press a kiss on her forehead. "Thank you, sweetheart."

Thrilled to bits, she took the bracelet from him and widened the two open edges before wrapping it around his right arm, before pressing the edges closer to fit him properly.

Chirag moved his arm up and down, admiring the bracelet, and liking it. "I've never worn a bracelet before." Or any other jewellery for that matter.

"I hope you'll wear it often."

He had no plans to take it off, ever. "I will," he promised, hugging her. "Thanks for making my birthday so memorable."

"We aren't done yet," she said, giving him a broad wink.

He laughed softly, ready to go with whatever she had planned for him. As far as he was concerned, this gift was truly the highlight of his thirtieth birthday.

C hirag found himself missing Shreya on his thirty-third birthday. He had decided to spend it right here in Delhi, as Shreya had no leave to join him anywhere for a holiday. Even their quarterly trips together had dwindled to twice a year.

He grimaced as he stared at the ceiling, recalling the last three birthdays, in Sydney, in Greece and the last year in Las Vegas. Tch! He missed her, badly.

"Good morning, Chirag; and happy birthday!" Chandrika greeted her son with a hug when he went down for breakfast. "What's your plan for today?" she asked, handing him a gift parcel wrapped in gold paper.

"Thank you, Mom," he said, kissing her cheek. "What have you got for me?"

"A scrapbook full of pictures, all prospective brides. You do remember your promise, no? That you will consider meeting girls when you complete thirty-two years." She lifted an eyebrow at him as she laid the breakfast table.

"Mom!" Chirag groaned, shutting his eyes. What the hell! How could he have forgotten he had made such a stupid promise? But then, the last four years had simply flown on wings, what with him building his agency from a one-million-dollar operation to a one-hundred-million-dollar one; and taking off on multiple trips around the world with his girlfriend.

"Happy birthday, Chirag," said Deven, stepping forward to give his son a hug. "Is everything alright?" he asked, noticing the weary expression on Chirag's face.

"Thank you, Dad," responded Chirag, returning his father's hug.

"You mother gave you our gift, already?" Deven lifted an eyebrow at Chandrika, who was biting her upper lip hard to stop herself from laughing. Turning back to his son, he saw the golden parcel in Chirag's hand before suggesting, "Why don't you open it?"

Chirag sat down on a dining chair to open the parcel, with a total lack of enthusiasm. Just as he was peeling back the gold paper, his gaze fell on the antique silver bracelet on his right forearm, a smile forming on his face as he recalled the time he had spent with Shreya in Sydney. He made it a point to wear the bracelet during all his waking hours, right from that day. With a sigh, he opened the cardboard box, his eyes going wide, his relief palpable when he saw the four books in it; the books he had been meaning to buy for himself. Lifting his head to look at his mother, he gave her a mock glare, smiling when she laughed outright.

"Mom!" he said, shaking his head at her, before getting up to hug her once again. "Thank you, Mom, Dad. This is exactly what I wanted for my birthday."

"Why were you glum earlier?" asked Deven, turning from his wife to his son and back to her again.

"That's because I told him his gift contained a scrapbook of pictures of prospective brides." Chandrika went into peals of laughter once again.

Deven began to laugh as well.

"You guys are being mean," declared Chirag, pretending to be miffed. Deep down, he was only too relieved the parcel hadn't contained anything like what his mother had told him. Phew!

Aadhira had her plan in place, and was glad that Providence was on her side when it became obvious that it wasn't possible for Shreya to meet Chirag for his birthday this year. Well, Aadhira liked Chirag Bhatia and respected the fact that he was the man her sister was in love with. But the man was an idiot, unable to notice what was right under his nose.

Aadhira had never missed the sadness in Shreya's eyes every time she returned from a trip with Chirag. The droop of her shoulders and the disappointment on her face were things which made Aadhira spend sleepless nights. But she never said anything to Shreya, all because she didn't want her sister to become more upset than she already was.

But this year, after speaking to the love of her own life—Reyansh Bhargav—Aadhira had come up with a concrete plan.

Aadhira and Reyansh were soon going to tie the knot, with the blessings of both their parents.

Ambika had not liked the fact that her younger daughter was getting married while the elder one continued to remain single. She spoke to Aadhira, "I understand that you are in love. And you're also twenty-three. But…" she sighed, turning to glance at Shreya who was sitting like a stone next to her sister. "Shreya, will you consider…?" Ambika stopped speaking when she saw her eldest born's head come up swiftly, a fiery expression in her eyes.

"Mom, you very well know that I don't want to marry anyone other than Chirag. And…"

"Of course, I understand that, Shreya. So, what's stopping you from doing exactly that? Do you want me to ask your father to speak to Chirag Bhatia's parents? I can even ask Rekha to speak to his parents on our behalf. He would be thirty-two, right? I'm sure his parents must be keen to get him married too."

"No, Mom. It can't work that way." Shreya got up to leave the room, not at all keen to discuss Chirag with her mother.

"Listen, Mom," said Aadhira, touching her mother's shoulder gently. "I have a plan…"

"For what?" asked Ambika, a complete lack of enthusiasm in her demeanour. She loved her children and gave them all the space they asked for. But she couldn't help feeling upset by Shreya's lack of faith in her matchmaking abilities.

"For Shreya. All I ask for is your co-operation." Aadhira explained her idea in a few sentences, glad to see a smile spread over Ambika's tense features.

"Are you sure it will work?"

"I'll make it work, Mom. You don't worry about it."

Ambika gave her younger daughter a nod, even as a sigh shuddered from the depths of her being. The end was worth the means, she supposed.

Aadhira left the hall to go to Shreya's bedroom. Their apartment in Durban was large and had eight bedrooms, other than a living room, a small sitting room, and a library. This was besides the kitchen and dining space; and not counting the multiple verandas.

"I'm so happy for you, Aadhi." Shreya gave her younger sister a smile which didn't reach her eyes.

"I know," said Aadhira, sitting next to her sister to hug her. "Why didn't you go for Chirag's birthday?"

Shreya shrugged. "I didn't feel like." She didn't want to admit that she felt heartbroken. At twenty-six, she had hoped that her steady—and only—boyfriend of four years would propose marriage. But it didn't look like Chirag was interested in a permanent relationship.

But then, he hadn't shown interest in any other woman since he met her. The gentle reminder from her mind was not of much help to Shreya. The long-distance relationship had been thrilling in the beginning. But it had begun to pall after the first couple of years. She knew Chirag was busy in building his business, and had managed to achieve all he had set out to do in the last four years. His company was doing extremely well, and he also had an able second-in-command these days.

As for herself, Shreya had put her idea of setting up her own yoga studio on hold. While she had enough money saved, she was still hoping to set it up in Delhi, the city Chirag was based in, rather than here in Durban.

Right now, she felt she was in limbo. Not meeting him for his birthday seemed to have hurt her more than it had bothered him. Shreya was guilty as if she had betrayed him in some way.

Aadhira watched the various expressions of pathos, guilt, anger, and frustration running across Shreya's face. That's when she decided not to take her sister into confidence regarding her plan. She planned to play

Cupid and there was no force on earth which was going to stop her.

"I love you, *di*," said Aadhira, getting up to kiss Shreya's forehead.

"I love you too," said Shreya, burying her face in Aadhira's shoulder and bursting into tears.

That night, Aadhira created a beautiful poster on a designing app. It was a wedding invitation. While the bridegroom's name was Reyansh Bhargav, she added Shreya's name in the place of bride. No, she felt no guilt about the blatant lie. If this didn't bring Chirag to his senses, then nothing else would.

It was time for the acid test! She simply couldn't sit back and watch her cheerful sister wallowing in misery. At least, now, Shreya would receive closure—either way.

18

Chirag Bhatia was spitting nails by the time he landed in Durban, at 5:35 AM local time. His body screamed with fatigue as he hadn't slept the whole night, even though he had travelled business class. It was a good thing that nothing seemed to impair Chirag's appetite and he had been well fed, during all meals. But it was more than twenty-four hours since he had got to know about Shreya's upcoming nuptials and his brain had been whirling crazily during that time.

As for Shreya, he was going to throttle her with his bare hands the moment he set eyes on her. And no, he was yet undecided about how he was going to deal with Reyansh Bhargav, the villain who had sprung out of nowhere.

It was a point in his favour that Aadhira had become a really good friend over the years. It was thanks to her that he had Shreya's address in Westville. He reached the twenty-eighth floor to ring the bell of the flat which had a hand painted board claiming that it belonged to the Udhas family.

Shreya went to open the door when the bell rang at seven am, wondering who was calling so early in the morning. Her mouth fell open in surprise, or was it shock, when she saw Chirag Bhatia standing outside, a small trolley bag at his feet.

"Are you going to invite me in?" he asked. No, he barked the question at her, without a smile on his face.

"Of course. Hello, Chirag! This is a surprise." She opened the door wider and stepped out of the way to let him in. If she had waited for his kiss, she might have probably waited until kingdom come. What was he doing here, at her home? That was when she realised they hadn't spoken to each other in the last forty-eight hours. Which was a first!

He didn't bother to return her greeting as he walked into the house as if he owned the place, his face rigid and unsmiling.

Shreya was relieved that she was the only one who was up, unless one counted Tina. But then, their house help was busy in the kitchen which was at the far back and was probably not even aware that someone was visiting them. Shreya didn't want her parents to meet him, not in the foul mood he was obviously in.

"We need to talk," said Chirag, turning to Shreya, his black eyes burning fiercely due to his seething temper which was on simmer at the moment.

"Of course. I'm sure you'd like to have some coffee. Let me go and get some."

"No, damn it! I don't want coffee." Chirag's voice was a roar as he glared at her down his patrician nose. He had thrust his hands into the pockets of his jeans. Otherwise, he wasn't so sure he might not throttle her with his bare hands.

Shreya straightened up to stand firmly in front of him, the expression in her eyes growing cold. "Fine then. But I want to have some. Why don't you go and sit in the veranda over there? I'll bring my coffee and join you soon." No one would disturb them there, not for at least an hour.

He gave her a ferocious glare before taking himself off in the direction of the veranda which was off the main hall of the flat. He leaned over the railing, not really registering the amazing view from the twenty-eighth floor. The whole area was lush with greenery and further beyond was the Natal Bay of the Indian Ocean. The strong and cool breeze which blew over, couldn't manage to calm down Chirag's raging temper.

He turned when he heard movement and saw Shreya step into the veranda, a tray containing two steaming mugs of coffee. She had changed out of the nightshirt she had been wearing when he arrived, her tousled hair combed back neatly and held at her slender nape with a scrunchy. She was wearing a pair of brief cotton shorts and a pink t-shirt. Curbing his urge to drool, he continued to glare at her.

"Why don't you sit down and enjoy the coffee while it's hot? I'm sure we can talk at the same time as we drink it." Shreya was logic personified, irritating him all the more.

He refused to sit down, deciding that towering over her from his superior height was bound to give him a better advantage. But he couldn't resist the aroma of freshly filtered coffee and Shreya sure knew how to mix it exactly the way he liked the brew. Lifting a cup, he sipped from it.

"So! What do you want to talk about?" asked Shreya, completely clueless about why he was here. She had no idea of the role Aadhira had played, in sending him a fake marriage invitation. Her whole body ached with the need to be in his arms, but the man in front of her was furious. What if it turned out to be like cuddling a grouchy bear?

Her very coolness set a spark to his anger and he exploded suddenly. Placing the half-drunk cup of coffee on the tray with a thud, he glowered at her. "Let me come directly to the point. When were you planning to tell me about the wedding?"

Shreya frowned up at him, wondering what he was talking about. Suddenly recalling that he and her sister were on excellent terms, she concluded he must have gotten to know about Aadhira's wedding and was asking her about it. She shrugged. "Whenever! Why? Are you planning to attend?" she asked, lifting a shapely eyebrow at him.

Chirag couldn't believe his eyes or ears. This woman was his girlfriend of four years. The one who was in a long distant relationship with him. They found it difficult keeping their hands off each other whenever they were in the same room. Even now, despite his anger towards her, all he wanted to do was to carry her to her bedroom and make hot, steamy love to her. How dare she ask him if he planned to attend her wedding with some other bastard?

He leaned down threateningly to place both his hands on the armrests of her chair, meeting her gaze head on. Shaking his head to clear off the sensation he felt of drowning in her big, brown eyes, he growled, "Did you hear yourself?"

She gazed back at him uncomprehendingly. All she wanted to do was to throw herself into his arms. She wanted—no, she needed—his lovemaking, right now. If he asked her to spend the rest of her life with him, even without marriage, she would agree. All she wanted to do was be with him, see him every day, wake up with him and go to sleep with him. Just now, she gave a small shake of her head. "I don't understand."

"How dare you ask me if I planned to attend the wedding?" he snarled, shaking her chair in frustration.

Shreya rolled her eyes to the ceiling and back to him. "Since it was you who brought up the subject. Listen, Chirag, this conversation is getting us nowhere. If you want to attend the wedding, then you are most welcome. It's on March 31st, right here in Durban." But she still didn't understand why he was here today, that too, without informing her prior to his visit. She definitely didn't believe he had meant it as a surprise for her. Not the way he was foaming at the mouth.

Chirag let go off the chair to turn away from her, putting some distance between them. No, he had never committed an act of violence against a woman. Never! But he was tempted, damn it! He was so tempted to shake Shreya out of her calmness. He wanted to shake her like a rag doll, until she agreed to… agreed to… what?

He stared out at the turquoise sea and the brilliant sun streaking its rays across the shimmering blue of the sky. How many ever deep breaths he drew to calm himself down, his temper refused to be diffused. Turning around with a jerk, he asked, "Do you love him?"

Shreya gave him a deep scowl. "Love who?" she asked, totally flummoxed. "Look Chirag, are you drunk?"

"I wish I was," he snarled, his black eyes spitting fire at her.

She ran her gaze down the length of his perfectly shaped masculine body, feeling a powerful urge to wrap her arms around him. They had had their share of tiffs, which had lasted less than a couple of hours at the most.

She truly couldn't understand the reason for his fury today. Lifting her gaze to his turbulent black eyes, she spoke to him softly, as if to a frightened wild animal. "Listen, Chirag. Why don't you sit down and tell me what's bothering you?" she invited, patting the chair next to hers.

He plonked down on the chair as he continued to glower at her, unable to believe his ears. Until this moment, he never knew Shreya had a deceitful nature. And he had been sure he had got to know her well these past years. "Why this sudden decision to get married?" he asked her.

"I… er… I don't get you. This isn't exactly a sudden decision, you see. She is twenty-three, and they have known each other for two years. Well, they both are sure they want to spend the rest of their lives together. That's why they are going ahead with marriage. Not everyone is stupid like us, are they?" she asked, a bitter twist to her beautiful lips.

Chirag shook his head a couple of times, trying to wrap his head around what she had told him. She had said it wasn't a sudden decision and she had known the man for two years. "But wait! Have you been seeing another man for the last two years? Like really? When we both have been having a hot, steamy, mind-numbing affair? Have you been two-timing me?" he barked, burning with jealousy. Oh yes, he did recognise the emotion which had been driving him mad from the moment he received Shreya's wedding invitation from Aadhira. All these years, he had believed Shreya belonged exclusively to him. That invitation had been a wake-up call of the worst order. He wasn't going to let any other man carry Shreya away from right under his nose.

Shreya scowled deeper than ever, trying to comprehend Chirag's words. Was he mad? Or was she hearing things? Imagining his words? She pinched her own arm, just to make sure she was not in the depths of a dream, maybe even a nightmare. In all the four years she had known him, she had never seen Chirag lose his temper, at least not to such an extent. She raised a hand in front of her, as if asking for a time out. As she gazed into his stormy gaze, she felt her own temper rising. She pushed her chair back to get up to her feet. "What the hell do you mean saying I've been two-timing you, you bastard?" she snarled, her brown eyes appearing like molten lava.

"Didn't you just say you've been seeing this guy for the last two years?" Chirag snarled right back.

"Which guy are you talking about? Don't be an idiot, Chirag. I've never looked at another man, and you well know it." While she was extremely angry with him, she hadn't missed the insecurity right at the back of Chirag's furious gaze.

"Then why the hell are you getting married to him?" Chirag shouted, jumping to his feet too.

"What? Marriage? Me? Are you mad?" Shreya was baffled by his words. Was he under the impression she was going to be married? Was that the reason why he had arrived on her doorstep so suddenly? But why would he think that? She shook her head to clear it, only it didn't help her one bit.

On the verge of letting rip, Chirag paused when he noticed the bewildered expression on Shreya's face. He took a deep breath, trying to recall their conversation. She had said… Shreya had mentioned…

She is twenty-three, and they have known each other for two years. Well, they both are sure they want to spend the rest of their lives together. That's why they are going ahead with marriage. Not everyone is stupid like us, are they?

Whaaaattttt!

Chirag ran the words in his mind for the third time as he paced the length of the veranda. Shreya must have been speaking about Aadhira. After all, it was her younger sister who was twenty-three. And Shreya's words were that Aadhira had known some guy for two years and they both had decided to tie the knot, because they wanted to spend the rest of their lives together. She had also mentioned that not everyone was stupid like the two of them—Chirag and Shreya.

A sudden smile lighting up his face, he came to a stop in front of Shreya, meeting her tempestuous gaze head on. "Shrey…"

"I think it's best if you left, Chirag." She spoke in a small voice, finding it difficult to stop it from cracking. She realised that their relationship was at an end. She simply couldn't carry on like this, not any more. It looked like after four years with her, he still couldn't trust her. How dare he ask her if she had been two-timing him?

"Shrey, listen. I'm sorry." He was ready to grovel at her feet. Anything to be back with her. He finally admitted to himself that he didn't want a life without Shreya in it. It had taken a false wedding invitation to make him come to his senses. He understood he had Aadhira to thank for that. It was obvious Shreya was not even aware of the role her sister had played in this drama.

"For what?" She crossed her arms over her heaving chest to glare up at him. No, she didn't plan to forgive him. What did it matter anyway? When nothing could convince him to make her his life partner?

"For being a complete fool. Not realising that I have been in love with you from the moment I met you for the first time."

Shreya, who had been planning to hold on to her anger until he left her alone, found herself melting on hearing his words. But, wait! She had to make sure he wasn't saying something in the spur of the moment. "That's something new! Are you sure you aren't making a fool of me?" she asked, giving him a cool glance from under her eyelashes.

"What would you like me to do?" He went down on his knees in front of her, taking her right hand in both of his. "Shreya! Sweetheart! I love you from the bottom of my heart. Yes, I needed one strong kick in my butt to admit to my feelings. But here I am, finally realising that I cannot live without you. Will you be mine?" When she didn't respond immediately, he wasn't above pleading, "Pretty please?"

Her heart picked up pace as she looked down into his beseeching eyes, his black gaze velvety and adoring. "Why suddenly?" she asked, refusing to budge from her high horse. Oh, it felt good to hear him beg. And her trampled heart needed the balm of his fervent appeal.

"Haven't you realised what happened?" he asked, a gentle smile on his face.

She shook her head slowly from side to side, curbing her instinct to throw her arms around his neck. The independent Aquarius wanted her pound of flesh. He owed her an explanation. While she was glad he had come to see her, she didn't like the idea that he had done it out of anger, and not because he had been dying to meet her.

Chirag stood up to gather her into his arms, pressing his mouth to her forehead in the gentlest of kisses. "Aadhira sent me a marriage invite on WhatsApp."

"Of course, I guessed as much. I only couldn't understand what set you off like a rocket. Are you angry because I didn't send you the invitation myself?" she asked him.

Chirag threw back his head and laughed uproariously, only to gasp when she punched a fist into his stomach. "Vixen," he declared, continuing to smile. Holding her fisted hand in his, he explained, "The bride's name on the invitation said, 'Shreya Udhas'."

Shreya, who had been trying to free her fist, let go of her effort to look up at him, her eyes and mouth wide open. "Come again?"

"You heard me," he said, his eyes dancing with mischief and joy.

"Did Aadhi give you the impression that I was getting married to Reyansh?" she asked, amazed at her sister's strategy.

"Yes," said Chirag, his mouth drooping at the corners. "She almost gave me a heart attack, you know?"

"Which was nothing less than what you deserved," said Shreya, spitefully, stepping out of his arms. "That's why you came running!" She couldn't help feeling disappointed.

"Shrey? Will you marry me?"

"I'll think about it," she said, turning away from him to walk to the railing, staring unseeingly at the vista in front of her.

"You don't mean that," he protested, stepping close to her to gather her into his arms once again.

"Why wouldn't I? I was always under the impression that you didn't want marriage. Now that you suddenly want it, am I supposed to agree immediately? How does that work?"

"That's simple. It will work because you love me and cannot imagine your life without me," he responded, a cocky grin on his face.

"Says who?" She pouted at the endearing expression on his face. Well, he had grovelled. And how! What more could she want from the man she loved from the depth of her heart and soul?

Deciding to chuck the words, he leaned down to capture her mouth in a deep and hungry kiss, exploring it thoroughly and satisfyingly. Finally, coming up for air, he repeated his earlier question, "Will you be mine?"

"Yes, yes, yes."

EPILOGUE

"Did you miss me?" Shreya's voice was a soft whisper as she stroked a finger down Jill's back. As always, the cats were piled one on top of the other as they slept in the living room of the Bhatias' bungalow. It was afternoon and the Bhatia parents were travelling. Only the newlyweds and the cats were at home.

It was only the day before yesterday when Chirag and Shreya arrived home after a two-week honeymoon in the Maldives.

She was sprawled on her front over the marble floor as she petted the cats, her brown eyes glowing with happiness as she chatted with Jack and Jill.

Jill purred in response, stretching her front paws even as she yawned widely, making Shreya laugh. While Jack was totally lost to the world as he slept on.

Chirag watched his wife of eighteen days with a joyous smile on his handsome face. It was the best decision of his life, getting married to Shreya. And he was so glad he didn't have to go rushing around the world to spend a few days with her, after prolonged months of separation. Yes, she was the love of his life and he was at complete peace for accepting the fact.

He lay down on the floor next to her, kissing a silky shoulder which was laid bare by the sleeveless vest she sported.

"Hey! You are awake." She turned to her side to smile at her husband, her eyes glowing with adoration. Reaching forward, she kissed his mouth, only to gasp when he pushed her on her back to lie down on top of her, returning her kiss passionately.

"Mmm…" She held his face in her hands, her thumbs stroking his ears while her mouth clung to his. She stroked his bare calves with her heels, glad he was wearing a pair of shorts and not much else, even as she ran her hands down his satiny back. "I love you, Chirag," she said, her lips brushing against his ear.

"Tell me again," he said, lifting his head to look down at her with desire-glazed black eyes.

"I love you, I love you, I love you." She nipped an ear lobe as she demanded, "Now it's your turn."

"I love you, sweetheart; to the end of the earth and back." Chirag nuzzled her neck, taking deep breaths as he inhaled her perfume—a blend of roses and all things Shreya. "Wanna go to bed?" he invited, taking her hand and placing it against his tumescent shaft.

She lifted heavy eyelids to gaze at him with melting brown eyes. "What's wrong with here?" she asked, lifting a challenging eyebrow.

He laughed softly, accepting her challenge to make love to her right there on the cool marble floor. He rolled around to his back, not keen for his darling wife's delicate frame to be pressed to the hard floor, even as he savoured every inch of her skin with his hands and mouth.

Shreya held on to his shoulders, gasping for breath as her husband made love to her, satisfying every whim of hers.

Satiated for the moment, Chirag lay next to his wife, wrapping his arm around her as he pulled her against his chest, spoon fashion, a deep sigh of satisfaction running through his body.

The Sagittarius man no longer had a commitment phobia, not now when he knew that Shreya, his Aquarius rebel, was the woman he wanted to live with for the rest of his life.

THE END

References

1. https://www.docdroid.net
2. http://sunsignsbylindagoodman.blogspot.in
3. http://www.astro.com
4. https://www.self.com
5. http://horoscopes.lovetoknow.com

Bibliography

1. *Love Signs* by Linda Goodman

OTHER BOOKS
BY
SUNDARI
VENKATRAMAN

WRITTEN IN THE STARS
BOOK 1
SCORPIO
SUPERSTAR
SUNDARI
VENKATRAMAN
AMAZON BESTSELLING AUTHOR

SCORPIO SUPERSTAR
(Written in the Stars Book 1)

Kollywood superstar Chandrakanth, also known as CK, is a true-blue Scorpio, communicating with his eyes and believing in showing more than telling.

His website and social media consultant Ranjini is a Piscean through and through, fiercely independent.

It is love at first glance for Chandrakanth when he meets Ranjini; so strong are his feelings that he proposes marriage on their second meeting. Ranjini, fascinated by his starry persona, gets swept off her feet. The two get married without much of the world knowing—including CK's aunt and his ex.

The two women set out to settle their scores on Ranjini who suddenly begins to feel a strain in her fairy tale marriage.

While passion reigns on the one hand, there's trouble in paradise on the other. Although CK is by her side, the Scorpio in him expects her to trust him implicitly. But can the Pisces in Ranjini accept him at his word?

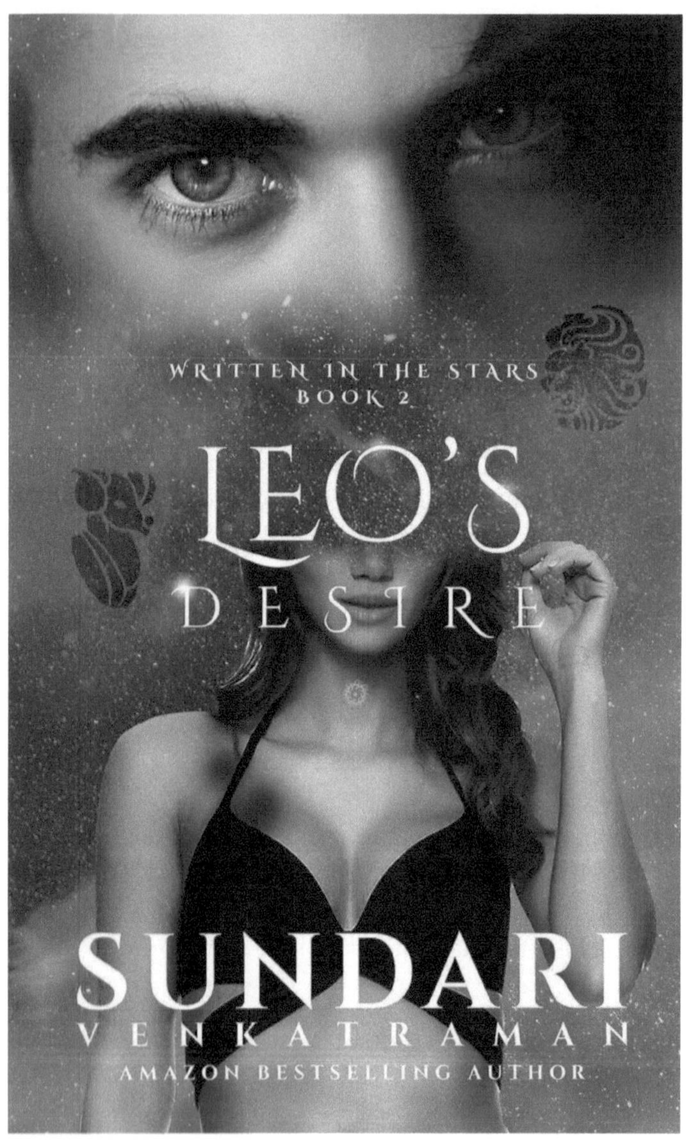

WRITTEN IN THE STARS
BOOK 2
LEO'S
DESIRE
SUNDARI
VENKATRAMAN
AMAZON BESTSELLING AUTHOR

LEO'S DESIRE
(Written in the Stars Book 2)

Twenty-four going on twenty-five, Nishaan Ahuja refuses to take life seriously. Intelligent and highly educated, he's slotted to become the Vice President of his father's multi-billion-rupee construction business. Only, the Leo man wants to live on his own terms. He takes the identity of Shaan and goes to work as a farm manager.

Chaahat finds a quick-fix cure to her plumpness as she's desperate to become a fashion model despite her parents' objections. The Aries woman is stubborn, determined and fiercely competitive. There's a hitch though. Her body refuses to cooperate as she continues to abuse it and she finds herself on the brink of a physical breakdown.

The Lion is a know-it-all and has to impart advice. Will the Lamb realise that it's all for her best?

Sparks fly in their love-hate relationship as Chaahat struggles to achieve her dreams with a lot of unsolicited help from Nishaan. Will the lovers be able to get together on their own terms, what with the distance which separates them; and their mammas doing their utmost to run interference?

WRITTEN IN THE STARS
BOOK 3
TAURUS
TEMPTATION
SUNDARI
VENKATRAMAN
AMAZON BESTSELLING AUTHOR

TAURUS TEMPTATION
(Written in the Stars Book 3)

Vidyut has a broken engagement behind him. But being the typical Taurus he is, he is unfazed when his fiancée from the arranged match hands his ring back to him.

Into his life walks Haasini, a successful entrepreneur in her own right. The Cancer woman brings a powerful dose of *joie de vivre* into the serious bull's hardworking life.

While the café owner struggles not to fall for the beautiful young lady, all because she is eight years his junior, Vidyut is unable to help himself when his heart refuses to listen to his logical mind. While Haasini has no qualms about admitting her feelings for him.

Just when things seem to fall in place for the couple, trouble brews from unexpected quarters, tearing them apart as it brings to the fore the jealous nature of the Cancer. While the bull moos loudly, the crab attempts to scuttle away.

Read the book to find out if they will ever find the happiness Destiny is keen to bring to the Taurus man and Cancer woman.

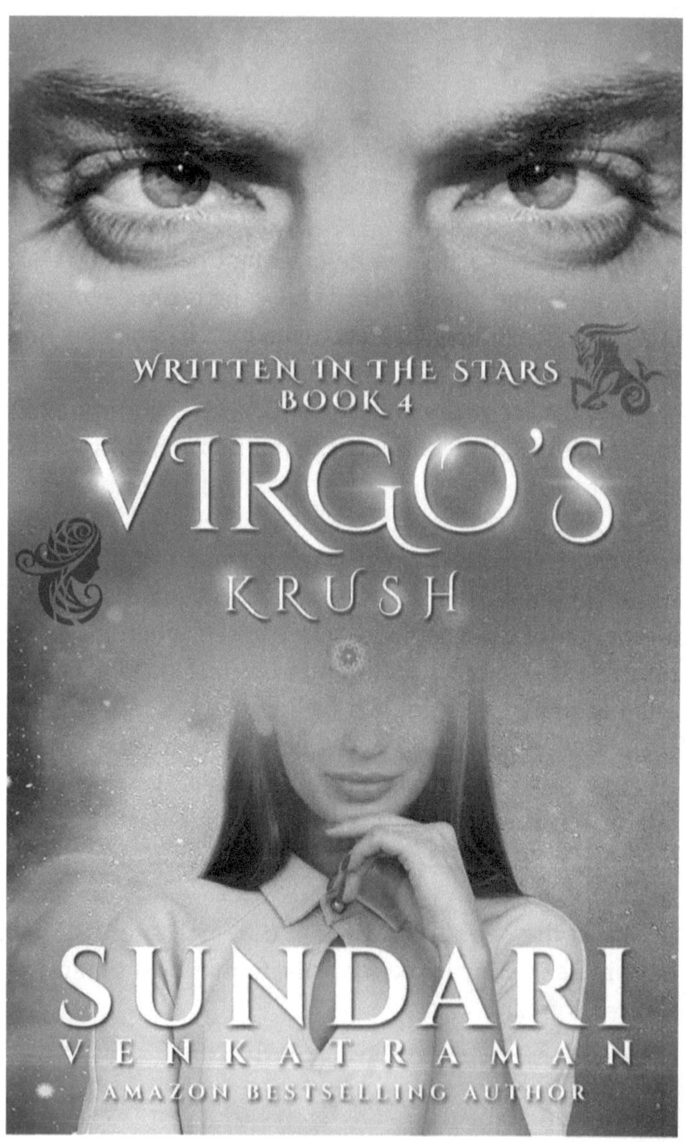
WRITTEN IN THE STARS
BOOK 4
VIRGO'S
KRUSH
SUNDARI
VENKATRAMAN
AMAZON BESTSELLING AUTHOR

VIRGO'S KRUSH
(Written in the Stars Book 4)

The gorgeous and intelligent Sanjana is a fiercely independent Virgo. Or is it only a front for the woman who wants to be loved?

As for Krish, the handsome and internationally famous photographer, is stunned to discover he is father to the two-month-old Kabir. Typically aware of his responsibilities, the Capricorn offers to marry the mother who he is deeply attracted to.

But the Virgo, already crushing on the Capricorn, wants all or nothing and refuses to settle for a loveless marriage.

He pushes, she resists...

It's like the proverbial Irresistible Force meeting the Immovable Object...

Shall the twain ever meet?

WRITTEN IN THE STARS
BOOK 5
LIBRA'S
FLAME
SUNDARI
VENKATRAMAN
AMAZON BESTSELLING AUTHOR

LIBRA'S FLAME
(Written in the Stars #5)

ipika Sanyal is an established, internationally renowned business woman, running a modelling agency. She is swept off her feet by the handsome Mudit, who simply refuses to take 'no' for an answer. The Libra woman is completely floored from the word go.

Mudit Trivedi is the financial director of a multi-million crore business. He is deeply attracted to Dipika the moment he sets eyes on her. The Gemini does not want to wait for even a moment before getting to know her better.

Things go really well for the two in the beginning, until his estranged family enters the picture. Dipika has never met a ruder person than his father. Will their relationship survive the strain placed upon it?

Read the book to find out if this hot and sizzling pair of Libra and Gemini can have a life together.

Connect with Sundari Venkatraman here:

Notion Press: Sundari Venkatraman Books

Amazon: Sundari Venkatraman Books

Website: https://www.sundarivenkatraman.in

Facebook: Author Sundari Venkatraman

Twitter: @sundarivenkat

Instagram: @sundarivenkatraman

Email: sundarivenkat@gmail.com